Just a Cowboy's Best Friend

Flyboys of Sweet Briar Ranch in North Dakota Book Two

Jessie Gussman

Published By: Jessie Gussman

This is a work of fiction. Similarities to real people, places, or events are entirely coincidental. Copyright © 2023 by Jessie Gussman.

Written by Jessie Gussman.

All rights reserved.

No portion of this book may be reproduced in any form without written permission from the publisher or author, except as permitted by U.S. copyright law.

Contents

Acknowledgements	V
1. Chapter 1	1
2. Chapter 2	12
3. Chapter 3	23
4. Chapter 4	31
5. Chapter 5	40
6. Chapter 6	46
7. Chapter 7	56
8. Chapter 8	65
9. Chapter 9	72
10. Chapter 10	80
11. Chapter 11	87
12. Chapter 12	94
13. Chapter 13	101
14. Chapter 14	107
15. Chapter 15	115
16. Chapter 16	123
17. Chapter 17	132
18. Chapter 18	148
19. Chapter 19	155
20. Chapter 20	164

21.	Chapter 21	169
22.	Chapter 22	176
23.	Chapter 23	186
24.	Chapter 24	193
25.	Just a Cowboy's Enemy	199
A Gift from Jessie		206

Acknowledgements

Cover art by Julia Gussman
Editing by Heather Hayden
Narration by Jay Dyess
Author Services by CE Author Assistant

Listen to a FREE professionally performed and produced audiobook version of this title on Youtube. Search for "Say With Jay" to browse all available FREE Dyess/Gussman audiobooks.

Chapter 1

June moved slowly through the house, her eyes caught by the wide expanse of beautiful blue sky outside her kitchen window. She stopped, letting the sight give a smile, both to her face and to her heart.

The silence of her house was almost audible.

It felt empty, abandoned, which gave her a hollow feeling inside as she thought this was the way her house would be all the time as soon as her youngest child graduated from high school.

"Meow."

She startled, then looked down, seeing Garfield walking silently across the dining room floor. He came over to her legs and pressed against them.

"Hey, Garfield," she said, taking a moment to bend down and scoop him up.

"Where's Tom?" she asked, after touching her nose to his and scratching his ears.

She looked around, but Tom was nowhere in sight. He was a little more shy, although certainly he was comfortable with June and typically only hid when her husband, Wayne, came home.

If, by some odd chance, Wayne was in the house, it could be days before June saw Tom.

But today, it was just her, and Tom would have no reason to hide.

The third and last of her three children had stayed overnight at a friend's house, because they were heading off to a rodeo early this morning.

When she was a young mom and wife, she used to dream of the day where she and Wayne would have the house to themselves on a Saturday morning.

They'd lie in bed and snuggle. Talk and laugh. Get up and watch the sunrise together, go out for breakfast, or just hang around the house enjoying each other's company.

They had been schoolgirl dreams, because nothing in her marriage had ever panned out the way she'd dreamed.

Wayne had never been interested in doing anything with the family or her. He'd gone to recitals and pageants and even church on occasion, when she begged and pleaded and prodded, sometimes even crying, although she had never used her tears as an instrument against him. Sometimes she just couldn't help herself.

She'd been lonely her whole marriage.

But she'd put on a brave front for the children.

But now, with just three years left for her youngest to be at home, she was looking at a life that stretched out before her, filled with good deeds, her work which she loved, and always looking to help others.

But still empty, alone, with no lifetime companion, even though she was officially married.

The longing hit her harder at some times than others. This morning had been hard. Just because of all the dreams that lay buried in dust. And because it would have been nice to have a companion on a Saturday morning.

She would be going to the community center to sit with her friends Helen and Miss April as Miss April shared wisdom from her almost fifty years of marriage.

Giving Garfield one last pat and looking around again for Tom, but not seeing him, she set Garfield down and made her way to the door.

Gathering her crafting bag and the things she had set out, she picked up the garbage that she had set by the door, which Wayne had walked by this morning on his way out to do whatever it was he needed to do, and walked out of the house, throwing the garbage in the garbage can by the shed before she got in her car and drove the short distance into Sweet Water.

Normally she was a big believer in looking ahead with anticipation and not looking back with regrets, but this morning, she wished so hard that she had made one major different choice in her life.

But while Wayne sometimes yelled at her, always blamed her for everything that went wrong, only talked to her when he didn't have anyone else to talk to or when he wanted her to do something for him, and only spent time with her when he didn't have any of his friends available, he had never cheated, not to her knowledge.

He lied to her a lot and definitely had a double standard. One for him and a higher, impossible one for her.

She wondered at times where she had gone wrong.

No one could say they hadn't been together long enough before they got married, since they'd dated for almost five years.

But the little things that nagged at her then had only gotten worse over time.

Maybe she was too trusting. Maybe he lied to her the whole time they dated, and she had just never noticed.

Pulling into the community center, she parked her car, grabbing her things and deliberately trying to pull her mind from where it had gone.

Wayne had done nothing that gave her a biblical reason to leave the marriage, and she had tried as hard as she could over the years to be the very best wife and mother she could, giving love and kindness and consideration, and getting nothing in return.

Coming here today was not to get advice on how to improve her marriage. She knew from experience that trying to talk to Wayne would only end up in an argument, because no matter how carefully she phrased things, any idea that their marriage might need to be improved was taken as an attack by him.

He was uninterested in seeing a marriage counselor or in hearing how he could be a better husband or father. He didn't think that she or the children should have needs outside of whatever he saw fit to bestow on them.

"Good morning," Miss April said as June stepped through the door, closing it behind her with her foot and shuffling the packages in her hand.

"It's a beautiful day," she said, smiling and meaning it. If she weren't coming here, if she didn't need to talk to Miss April, she would be outside in her garden. It was that kind of day.

But more and more, she'd been thinking about leaving Wayne, even though she knew the only biblical reason for divorce was fornication.

Not neglect, not an abandonment of duty, if the husband didn't love his wife the way Christ loved the church and gave himself for it, the wife was not given permission to leave. Just as the husband was not given permission to leave if the wife didn't submit or obey.

It was up to each partner to keep their end of the marriage.

Still, it was discouraging to think that she would spend the rest of her life being ignored and neglected, unable to find a partner who truly cared about her, while basically being a single woman who did a man's laundry.

If she was going to be single, she didn't want the extra laundry to do.

Knowing that mindset wasn't biblical, she came, maybe not eagerly, to listen to what Miss April said each week, trying to do the right thing, the biblical thing, instead of the thing that she wanted to do.

After all, she wasn't supposed to live her life to make herself happy. She was supposed to live her life to glorify God. And if in order for her to glorify God she had to love someone who was unlovable and stay with them, to serve them and continue to be a blessing to them, even when she got nothing from them in return, that's what she wanted to do.

In theory.

In reality, her heart wanted romance. Or at least a gentle love. A soft touch, a kind word, companionship, kindness, smiles and laughs and family time together.

She swallowed, keeping the bright look on her face, wanting with all her heart to let her life be directed by God and not by her schoolgirl dreams. Even if she was in her early fifties.

"June, I could hardly wait for you to get here. Miss April was talking about the foundation of a marriage being friendship. I wanted her to keep talking, but I didn't want you to miss anything. So, I have been pacing back and forth watching out the window for you to pull in."

"I'm sorry. I thought I would be early. I had the house to myself this morning."

"Your husband already left?" Helen asked, knowing the history, at least some of it, and that her husband typically didn't spend any more time with her than what he absolutely had to.

"Yeah. He always says when you own your own business, you never get a day off."

Not even Sundays. Sometimes he would go to church with her and the kids, but he'd pull his phone out and play on it the entire time the preacher was talking. There was never any chance that he might hear anything that would cause him to look at his own life. Not just because he was playing on his phone, but because Wayne already thought he was perfect, and the idea that someone could say something that might improve him—he would say a person can't improve perfection, laugh, and then live exactly that way. Like he was perfect, and there was no improving perfection.

Miss April came over as June put her things down and gave her a hug. "How are you doing?"

"I'm doing well," June said, and she felt that was the honest answer. She didn't come here to complain about her husband, although she had mentioned a few of the facts.

She came to listen to Miss April, and she didn't want to turn it into a whining session. After all, the Bible said if they bite and devour each other, take heed that they be not consumed one of another.

She didn't want to bite and devour her husband, no matter how unkind he was to her. She did, however, want advice on how to do the best she could. Be the best Christian she could. So that others might see Jesus in her.

Miss April didn't say anything as she pulled back, looking deep into June's eyes. There was compassion in her gaze, as there always was. "We were talking about being best friends before you get married. Or marrying your best friend."

"I think that's a really good idea."

Miss April nodded, helping June unpack the bags that she brought, taking her hot glue gun over to the table and plugging it in. "We're taught that we need to have romantic sparks. Attraction and all the tingly feelings, and those are nice, but marriage is so much more than tingly feelings. You need to like the person you're married to."

June sighed to herself, wondering if that was her husband's problem. Wayne didn't like her.

She had to admit, the longer they were married, the less she liked him. Twenty years ago, when they'd only been married for a decade, he still seemed to try to be a good person. To be someone who cared a little about her, at least.

But it seemed like he totally quit trying in the last decade.

While she had redoubled her efforts.

Although she had to admit in the last year or so, she felt like she had given up.

"It's hard to be friends with someone who doesn't want to be friends with you," she said, hoping her words sounded casual.

Miss April settled herself on her end of the table. "That's a great point. And someone might be your friend now, but they might decide that they don't want to be your friend ten years from now. There's not much you can do about that."

"Like when your spouse wants to leave. There's not much you can do about it. That's not your decision."

"Exactly. It's not." Miss April nodded. "But what is your decision is how you're going to live today. If you still have your spouse with you, are you being kind to them? Are you treating them the way you would want to be treated, no matter how they treat you? Are you looking for ways to bless them? Or are you more interested in looking outside your home to find people to bless?"

"There is nothing wrong with looking outside your home, as long as you're taking care of the people in your home first," June said, although she knew both ladies knew it. She was just saying that maybe as a reminder to herself. A reminder that if she did the best she could for her husband, which mostly consisted of washing his clothes and cleaning his house and raising his kids since he typically wasn't around, then she was free to look outside the house to see other people she could do kind things for.

"I actually had a purpose behind talking about being friends before you get married," Miss April said, with a sheepish look at Helen.

"I knew it!" Helen said, beaming.

Helen was a little bit younger than June, but June was pretty sure she was also in a marriage where she and her husband had, at the very least, drifted apart.

"I hope you're thinking about what I'm thinking about," June said to Miss April with a smile.

Miss April raised her brows. "Matchmaking?"

June nodded slowly, her eyes feeling like they were glowing as she and Miss April exchanged a look.

Ever since Sweet Water's lead matchmaker, Miss Charlene, had gotten married, she hadn't been as involved in matchmaking as she had when she was single.

Helen squealed. "Who?"

Miss April smiled at both women, then she raised her brows. "Best friends?"

That was all she needed to say before June knew exactly who she was talking about.

"Deuce and Teagan," June and Helen said at the same time.

Miss April nodded. "Exactly."

Just as quickly as her excitement had spiked, June deflated, staring at the glass beads in front of her. "But they really are best friends. I mean, they've been best friends for a decade or more."

"More, for sure," Miss April said, nodding again. "But they are prime candidates for a match. Because they're such good friends. They know each other inside out, and they have that great foundation that is solid and strong and perfect to build a marriage upon."

It was the kind of foundation that June thought she had had, but she realized, looking back, that it was what she *wanted*, not what she *had*. She had looked at what she had through rose-colored glasses, trying to make it check all the boxes she wanted, when it really hadn't.

How she wished she would have had someone to tell her that she was going about it all wrong. But she had longed for intimacy and romance, and she hadn't been interested in having a career, as so many other women seemed to want. She wanted to be someone's wife, someone's best friend, someone's lover. The person who kept the house and worked behind the scenes to make everyone happy, doing everything she could to make their lives better in whatever way she could.

"They would be a perfect couple, but how are you going to get them to see that?" June asked.

Miss April grinned, a grin that was sly and competent at the same time. "You're going to help me."

June blinked. "Me?"

She was the last person alive qualified to do any kind of matchmaking. Even when her children asked her for relationship advice, she always said as little as would appease them. What did she know about relationships? Just what didn't work. Just that you couldn't put one hundred percent effort in when another person put zero and think you were going to have something worthwhile.

Or you could put one hundred percent in, but if the person you were married to was not a good person, it felt like casting your pearls before swine, only when you made a vow, you had to keep it. It was a covenant, not something that could be broken just because someone felt like it.

"Yes."

"Are you going to tell us what you're doing?" Helen asked, sounding eager, her hands holding her flowers, but they stilled on the table, and she hadn't even begun to start arranging the wreath she was working on.

"Edgar and I will be celebrating another anniversary in a few months, so we're going to Italy for three weeks."

"Wow!" June exclaimed. "That's fantastic!"

"I've never been, and I can't wait. Edgar is not quite as eager, but he loves me and knows I've wanted to go my entire life and haven't been able to, so he's doing it for me." Miss April beamed, and June's heart warmed. It was obvious that Miss April adored her husband, and if Edgar, who had lived in the West all of his life and was perfectly happy to never set foot out of the state, had agreed to go to Italy, he must be completely infatuated with his wife.

June tried not to compare that to her own marriage where her husband wouldn't even stop at the grocery store to bring a gallon of milk home for her when she had three small children.

It had been years since she'd asked him to do anything for her, because it was just setting herself up for disappointment.

"We've booked our tickets, and we even have a tour set up. I'm going to see Rome, the Coliseum, and dip my toes in the Mediterranean Sea. We also have almost an entire week of doing nothing but relaxing at this amazing villa. It's the trip of a lifetime."

June and Helen exchanged a smiling glance at Miss April's dreamy tone. There was no doubt that this trip was something she was looking forward to in a huge way.

After a bit, June said, "I'm not sure I understand how your trip plays into getting Teagan and Deuce together."

"Oh." Miss April blinked and seemed to bring her mind back down to their level. "I'm sorry. I can't believe I'm getting to go to Italy after all of these years. I get a little carried away about it."

"I hadn't noticed," June said, her voice holding humor and a heavy dose of sarcasm.

Miss April smiled even broader. Then, as though she were adjusting her mind to focus on the subject at hand, her face grew a little more serious. "I need someone to babysit my cats while I'm gone."

"You don't have cats," Helen pointed out immediately.

"I know. That's where you come in. June, I need to borrow your cats."

"...Sure. If this is going to help get Teagan and Deuce together, I know my cats will be all for it."

"I have a parakeet you can borrow," Helen offered.

Miss April laughed a little. "I'll take you up on that,"

"I'm not quite sure I see the connection just yet." June tried not to push, but she was anxious to see how this whole matchmaking thing was going to work. She didn't understand how a trip to Italy, a couple of cats, and a parakeet could end up helping Teagan and Deuce realize that they liked each other for more than friends.

"I'm going to ask Teagan to catsit. And parakeetsit apparently," Miss April added hastily, lifting a brow.

Then, she lowered her voice and told Helen and June exactly how she saw everything playing out.

June had to admit the plan was brilliant.

Chapter 2

"That is such a cool place. I've always wanted to stop and look at it."

Deuce leaned forward and looked out the windshield to where Teagan pointed. "That old abandoned house?" Vines covered the side of the weather-beaten boards, and the roof looked like it was ready to cave in at any moment.

"Yeah. Someone lived there once. Doesn't it just kind of draw you in a sad and almost eerie kind of way?"

"No. Can't say I ever even had the thought that I might want to stop," Deuce said as he put his foot on the brake and put his turn signal on as well.

"I didn't mean we had to stop!" Teagan said immediately, glancing over at him across the bench seat in his pickup.

"Do you have somewhere else you need to go today?"

It was Saturday, and she'd ridden with him two hours north of Sweet Water while he delivered a horse that he'd trained to the fellow who had bought him.

He had another pair of horses to pick up, and Teagan had just come along to keep him company. She knew he preferred to have her along on long trips like this. It made the time go faster, and he couldn't think of anyone else he'd rather be with.

The least he could do was to stop at some rundown, old house just to satisfy her curiosity.

He'd never be able to go by this house again without thinking of Teagan. He had no idea where she came up with some of the crazy things she thought of. But it was enough for him to know that her brain just worked differently than his did, and somehow they seemed to be compatible anyway.

Or maybe they'd just figured out long ago that different didn't mean bad, and they enjoyed the things that made each other unique.

He didn't know. He didn't spend much time thinking about their relationship, just that Teagan was odd sometimes, and he liked her that way.

"Oh, my goodness! I can't believe we're actually stopping." The excitement in her voice was obvious and a little contagious.

He tried to see the old, rundown house from her eyes. True, someone probably had lived there once.

"I wonder why they had to leave it? Why did they sell? Why would they just walk away from their home?"

"You face the North Dakota winter each year, the dark and the cold and the constant wind. I can't believe you even asked that." He didn't mean it to be mean, just to his mind, there were a million reasons why people would leave. It was why people stayed that sometimes made him wonder.

"Maybe she was a woman with eight kids and her husband died and she couldn't afford to feed them, so she had to farm them out and turn to prostitution in order to survive." Teagan's voice held a bit of whimsy.

"That's cheerful."

She shot a glance at him, the kind she usually did when he was being goofy when she was in one of her nostalgic moods.

"It's true." He defended himself.

"Or maybe some man lost his wife, and he couldn't stand to face life without her, so he left the home and farm that they'd worked on all their lives together and walked into the ocean, never to return."

"More likely, he got to the ocean and was so tired from walking all that distance he lay down and drowned."

"Or their farm was so prosperous that they were able to walk away from it without having to sell it, and they moved to Florida, enjoying the sun and the sand and the surf and never saw another snowflake in their entire lives. And they spent their last years holding hands and staring into each other's eyes, thinking about how blessed they were to have each other."

"Or they left the house and went to Florida because they couldn't stand the snow, and she found someone richer, with more hair, and less belly, and left her husband alone in a nursing home while she jetted off to Hawaii before settling in a villa in France with her new love who happened to own a vineyard and a winery."

"No. Someone who lived in North Dakota would never be happy in France on a winery."

"Why not? Actually, living in North Dakota could drive you to want to live on a winery."

"You love it here." She grabbed her door latch and yanked. But she didn't get out until he answered her.

"That's because my best friend is here. I still think we ought to move to Arizona or Texas. Someplace where it's hot more than it's cold."

She laughed, knowing he was joking, mostly.

It was true about his best friend. She was the best thing about North Dakota. And if she ever decided to move somewhere else, she wouldn't have to twist his arm to go with her. Mississippi sounded like a good spot.

He got out of his door and, instead of walking around the front of the truck, walked around the back, looking in the trailer and checking on his horses.

"Hey, there, pretty girl," he said softly, sticking a hand up so the mare could sniff his fingers.

The gelding was farther back, and he checked on him too, murmuring a few more words.

Rather than walking over to the house herself, Teagan had walked to the back of the trailer, knowing he would check on his horses, and was waiting for him there.

"They look good?" she asked.

"They'll be fine. It's cool enough that they can stand for a bit."

Teagan loved horses as much as he did, but her love involved watching them and doing whatever he told her to do with them. She didn't work with them much, just hung out with him and helped him where he needed it.

He was the same with her baking business. Hanging out at the farmers market or at her house on Monday night, rolling out pie dough or stirring a fruit and sugar mixture for pies.

He had to admit he wasn't much of a baker, but it was like anything else, it was fun as long as Teagan was doing it with him.

The wind blew, rustling the grass and making something creak from the direction of the house. Maybe a piece of metal on the roof was loose?

"How old do you think it is?"

"I don't know. We could probably find out. There are probably records at the courthouse. Less than a hundred years?" He was guessing, because he really had no idea. But it was a wood-sided house, so it couldn't have been that long. The paint had long since worn off, and the boards were dark gray.

Eventually they'd rot, and the entire thing would fall in.

Weeds grew up around the porch, and scrub brush poked through a few cracks in the porch floor.

They stood at the bottom of the porch steps.

"They look sturdy enough to walk on." He studied the boards, deciding he was right about their ability to hold their weight before looking overhead to make sure the roof wasn't sagging to the point where it was going to fall on him when he walked up.

"Are you sure it's safe?" Teagan asked.

"No. But isn't that the point of an adventure? You don't know exactly how it's going to go, you just embark on it because you know it's going to be fun."

"I thought it would be fun to come over here and feel it."

There she went, doing something that was very different from him. He didn't *feel* things. He observed them. What he could see, what he could hear, what he could touch, what he could figure out.

She had some kind of way of observing the world that he didn't, through some kind of feelings, is the only thing he could figure out.

It wasn't bad, just different.

"You go ahead and feel it, I'll keep an eye on the ceiling." They worked well together, when they respected each other's differences.

She gave him a grateful glance, probably knowing exactly what he was thinking.

That was something else that was uncanny about her. She could almost read his mind. Especially if she put her mind to it. That wasn't to say that sometimes she didn't totally miss the mark, because she did.

But so did he. She helped him learn to be more considerate, even though it wasn't something that came naturally to him. He just had to use the personality he had, observing things, taking in facts, in a way that helped him be considerate to others.

Like now. He knew she could get engrossed in what she was doing and not pay attention to danger. So he could help her do what she wanted and keep her safe while she enjoyed herself and didn't have to worry about little details like the roof caving in.

"Oh, man. This is so cool," she breathed, looking in the window where the glass had long ago broken out.

Keeping an eye out for anything that seemed unusual, he said, "They didn't even take the dishes off the counter. Just left them."

"I can't believe they're still here. That people didn't cart them off."

He supposed it was possible that people had squatted in the house after the original owners left, and those were their dishes. But they looked old, if not antique. A 1950s or 60s type of bowl.

"It wasn't someone's good china," he said.

"No. Not to us. But maybe it was good to them."

"Then they probably would have found a way to take the good china with them."

"Maybe," she said, just standing, like she could feel the spirits of the people who used to be there or what was left of their presence.

Like the walls of the house could talk to her. He didn't think it was magic or anything of that nature, just something that she could pick up, almost like people's feelings. She had often said that walking into a room with a lot of people was painful, just because she felt all of the pain in the room.

Normally Teagan was a happy person, who loved to joke and laugh, but that hid her sensitive side.

She was smiling, though, as she looked at him.

"Feels like there was a lot of happiness here." Her eyes glowed. She put her lips together. "I'd really like to go in."

He looked again at the roof and ducked his head in the window, seeing the plaster falling down from the ceiling and lying in crumbling pieces on the floor.

"I'll walk in and see what I think," he offered.

"I don't want anything to happen to you," she said, her voice holding serious tones, before she grinned. "Who would I hang out with if you ended up getting a broken leg or something?"

"You'd still hang out with me."

"I know. Only then I'd be stuck inside, probably sitting beside you while you lay on the couch and complained. I'd never hear the end of it, that you broke your leg because of me."

"If I promise that there's a five-year expiration date on the complaining and blaming, would you be okay with that?"

She pretended to think about it. "Two and a half."

"Four and a quarter."

"Three and nine tenths."

"Deal."

"Okay. But be careful anyway. Because that's still a long time to have to listen to you complain."

He chuckled, putting a hand on the door.

Before he could open it, Teagan's phone rang out with her ringtone, "Jingle Bells."

"Normal people don't have a 'Jingle Bells' ringtone on their phone in June."

"It's Christmas in June," Teagan said with a grin, pulling her phone out.

He turned back to the door as she said hello, wondering if it would be locked. He didn't think he'd go as far as breaking down the door to satisfy her curiosity, but he might try to jiggle the latch if he had to.

Teagan didn't say anything for a bit, and then she said, "I'm with Deuce right now. We're bringing horses home. But I can be there before noon, unless we run into something." She held a warning note in her voice, which made Deuce turn around.

She had the look on her face that said that if he got hurt, he would delay them from doing whatever it was that whoever was on the phone wanted them to do so he should do his very best to be careful.

He had no trouble reading that look. He'd seen it, in all of its various forms, multiple times throughout the years.

He wasn't sure what it was, but he thought it was a man thing that when a woman looked at him with a look that said, *be careful and don't do anything stupid*, it just made some part of him want to not be careful and do the stupidest thing he could possibly think of.

All the while telling himself that he wasn't being stupid and that he was being careful.

At least, that's the way Teagan explained what happened when she gave him that look.

He recalled all of that as he opened the door, the knob turning easily in his hand. Not locked after all. The floor wasn't quite level, and the door got stuck about halfway open, but then it pushed easily the rest of the way, swaying a bit, like the floor dipped down.

He stepped in.

Teagan would feel whatever was in the room, but he just saw a lot of mess on the floor, plates on the counter, a chair with one rung broken off and another upset on the floor, with one leg missing.

Interesting that the dishes had made it, but the chair hadn't.

An old refrigerator sat in the corner.

He could hear Teagan's voice. It sounded like she was hurriedly getting off the phone, probably so she could chase him, and he had to grin at that.

Maybe that was why her look made him do all the crazy things. Just because he enjoyed having her come after him, giving him a hard time, worrying about him, and dragging him off. He wasn't sure why that was so enjoyable, but he kinda looked forward to it.

In the meantime, he put his hand on the refrigerator door. It was one of those old ones that latched from the outside. The kind that if someone got inside the refrigerator and the door closed behind them, they wouldn't be able to open it from the inside and would suffocate unless someone let them out.

Maybe it was that thought that made him hesitate as he started to pull down on the latch.

He didn't want to open the refrigerator door and find a pile of bones.

That might put a new spin on their theory as to why people left the house.

That, and what the house had been used for over the years.

"If there are bones in there, I'll be waiting in the pickup." Teagan's voice came from just over his shoulder, and he had to force himself not to jump.

"You're done with your phone call?" he asked, hesitating, only because he was curious as to what she was going to do when they got home. At least, that's what he told himself. It had nothing to do with the fact that there might be bones in the refrigerator.

"Yeah, it was Miss April. She wants me to come into the community center when we get home or before lunch. I can help you unload your horses and hang out for a bit. As long as I'm in Sweet Water by noon."

"We have plenty of time."

"That's what I thought." She jerked her chin at the refrigerator. "Are you sure you want to open that?"

"There might be a drink in here. Aren't you thirsty?"

"No. I'm not. Not even a little."

"You don't want me to open the door?"

"Um... Yeah. I do. But I'm a little afraid. Does that make sense?" She laughed, a combination of nerves and fear. "I know you said that's one of the things that drives you crazy. The way I feel two things at once."

"It doesn't drive me crazy. It just makes you weird."

"You're weird because you don't."

He was usually much more of a straight line than she was. And they'd come to grips with that over the years.

"Are we going to count to three?" she asked, excitement laced with fear in her voice.

"Nah," he said just before he yanked the door open.

She gasped, the way he thought she would, but then they were both disappointed. Or relieved. Depending on one's perspective.

Since there was nothing in the refrigerator except two metal racks. And a rusted-out pile of metal that could possibly have been a coffee pot or water pitcher at one time.

"Oh." Teagan's voice held disappointment.

"Seriously? You're disappointed because there are no bodies in here?"

"No. Of course not."

"You sound defensive. Like you are, but you're defending yourself because you know that you shouldn't be."

"That's ridiculous. If anyone is disappointed, it's you. After all, you're the one that's morbid between the two of us."

"I wouldn't say that."

"You're the one who's opening the door. If I were here by myself, I wouldn't have even come in the house." She paused. "Probably not."

"It's a good thing you aren't here by yourself. I don't like the idea of you wandering around without someone watching out for you. You have a tendency to go around with your head in the clouds."

"That's why I cart you around everywhere I go. It keeps me from doing anything dumb."

"So glad I can be of service."

They both knew he didn't mind, and neither one of them said anything more as he closed the door, latching it.

"Crazy that the latch still works, and the refrigerator is still here after what has to have been decades, at least."

"I know. It probably would even work if we could turn the electricity on in the house."

"It seems like these old refrigerators are pretty much indestructible."

She grunted, and they moved away, looking around, with Teagan casting a long glance at the stairs before they moved to a doorway.

"I don't think that's a good idea."

"I know. I think going up would be really cool, but I think you're right. It's one thing to nose around the bottom story. It's another thing to be up in the air and have something collapse."

Without saying anything more, they walked out, with Teagan waiting while he closed the door.

"Satisfied?"

"I guess. It leaves me with a little bit of a longing. Just...a feeling of not quite déjà vu but just like there's something here."

He didn't say anything, knowing that she often felt things he didn't and things that he couldn't explain. He just had to let them go, knowing he would probably never understand.

They walked off the porch together, with Deuce knowing that he would never have stopped if it hadn't been for Teagan.

He thought, not for the first time, that being with her pulled him out of his bubble in ways he couldn't even imagine but that he appreciated. Having Teagan in his life as his best friend was definitely one of the main things he thanked God for every day.

Chapter 3

Deuce stood at the corral fence looking at the pair of horses he'd brought home, a pleased expression on his face.

"They're a beautiful pair," Teagan said, admiring the horses from beside him as they cautiously sniffed the newcomers.

"I agree. The guy wanted just a little bit of nothing for them. They're pretty, but they'll need a lot of work."

"After seeing how hard it was to get them on the trailer, it's obvious they need to be worked with, and that's going to take a lot of time."

"It will, but they're both smart and have nice coloring. I'll be able to get a lot out of them once they're trained."

She nodded in agreement. Both of them knew the horses would probably end up going out of state. There weren't many people in North Dakota who could afford to pay what he was going to be asking for the team.

"A year?" she asked.

"At least. Depends on how much time I have to spend with them, but yeah. Maybe two."

It would be worth it. He was never going to get rich working with horses, but he helped out as tech support for his family's construction warehouse wholesale business and kept up with the work on the ranch as well.

Teagan often helped him. Not with the tech support stuff, since she had no idea about any of that, but with the ranch work.

His three sisters were friends of hers as well, and they all worked in the family business.

Deuce was her age and her best friend though.

Horses were his passion, so while she loved to watch them and enjoyed riding, she spent more time with them than she normally would just because it was something he loved. After all, he didn't hesitate to help her with her baking business if she needed it.

The horses trotted over to the other side of the corral, their noses in the air, their manes and tails blowing in the wind.

"They are gorgeous," Teagan said softly. Just enjoying whatever it was about horses that stirred people's souls.

"Yeah." Deuce didn't say anything more, and he probably wouldn't. The more emotional he felt, the less he said.

Usually they goofed off and joked together, but when it came to horses, Deuce could be very serious.

"You should keep these for yourself," she said, surprising herself since she didn't typically make suggestions like that.

She could feel him stiffen beside her, and then he looked over at her. "You like them that much?"

She lifted a shoulder. "They're pretty. I think they suit you. I think you like them that much."

He grinned a little, then he shook his head. "No. Don't even try that. We both know you're the one that gets attached to things. I love them, love training them, then I'm ready to get on with the new challenge."

"There were several horses that you'd have liked to have kept over the years. Probably wish you would have kept."

"That's true. But you're the one that always cries when they leave."

"I do not."

"That's why you quit getting out when you go with me to deliver them? Because you can't stand to see them go. I wondered why you sat in the truck today."

"Well, I didn't cry." It was true; if she got out when he delivered them, she ended up bawling like a baby. It was embarrassing.

"If you want to keep them, we'll do that. We'll make them our horses."

"Nah. If you can make a lot of money with this team, I don't want you to forgo that just for me." Plus, surely someday he was going to find someone to settle down with. And what would they do with their horses then?

She didn't say anything about that though, because that thought made her sad too. She'd be happy for Deuce if he found his lifetime love, but she'd probably bawl like a baby the same as she did when the horses left. Because nothing would ever be the same between them again.

"I better get going. I was supposed to be in Sweet Water by noon, and I'll be pushing it as it is."

"Want me to come with you?"

"I know you're eager to get started here. And I can't imagine what they want me to do, but I'm sure it has something to do with helping someone either shop, or clean, or do yard work. I can handle that by myself."

"Be sure to call me if you need me," he said, his gaze already going back to the horses. Which made her smile. It was obvious his heart was totally in what he did, and he loved it.

"I'll do that."

She smacked his shoulder gently as she turned and walked away. It didn't take long to drive into Sweet Water, and she pulled into the community center at five to twelve.

Miss April looked up as she walked in, and Miss June, who had been speaking, stopped midsentence. Miss Helen, sitting at the far end of the table, smiled and continued working with her flowers.

"Good morning, ladies. And it is still morning," Teagan said as she held up her phone, facing it toward them, even though she knew it was likely that none of them could see that she made it with five minutes to spare.

"Good morning," Miss June said.

"How about I just say good afternoon and get a jump on things?" Miss April said, with a twinkle in her eyes.

Teagan laughed. "That's fine, or you can just say hello, if you can't wait for four more minutes until the clock strikes twelve."

"Technically, it wouldn't be afternoon until 12:01."

"Actually, once it hits 12, one second later it's after 12, right?"

"I think this is something we could debate."

Teagan loved coming in and bantering with the ladies. There was just something relaxing and comforting about them. All mothers, all older women, older being relative. In their forties, fifties and seventies, compared to her thirties.

"So, I take it you guys are going to put me to work," she said easily as she grabbed a chair and sat down at the table where they were working.

"You could say," Miss April said easily.

"Miss April has an exciting adventure planned, and she needs your help."

"An exciting adventure?" Teagan asked, thinking about the abandoned house that Deuce and she had explored today. Every time she drove by it, she had wondered what it was like inside. How it would feel, mainly, although she was curious as to how it would look as well. He had satisfied both of those questions for her, and it was something she probably would never have done on her own. Not everyone had a best friend who did everything with them and who was game for crazy ideas like Deuce always was.

"Honeymoon," Miss June said, giving Miss April a glance.

"That's right. Both are correct. I'm going on an adventure, and a honeymoon, to Italy. With Edgar."

"Wow. That sounds like a lot of fun." Teagan couldn't say she ever really wanted to leave her home country. There were so many fun things to see right where she was. Like explore abandoned houses, and care for beautiful teams of horses that needed to be trained. There was the wide North Dakota sky, and the plains, with the first fresh snow of the season on them. She didn't need to go to another country to be perfectly happy with all there was to see and do right where she was.

Although she didn't begrudge anyone who wanted to. She supposed people were just different that way. Different in the way they saw the world, different in the way they wanted to experience it. Different in the things they loved and longed for. Differences didn't make someone wrong, it just made them...different.

"I'm expecting it to be. And I'm excited about it. I'll be gone for three weeks." Miss April set the material she had been sewing down on the table and turned to fully face Teagan. "Three weeks is a long time, and I didn't want to have to board my darling kitties. They're so sweet, and they get upset any time their schedule is disrupted. I was hoping that you might be interested in coming to kittysit them while I'm out of town."

Miss Helen cleared her throat, and Teagan glanced over before looking back at Miss April.

"There's also my parakeet. She's a sweet thing. So cheerful and darling, but the cats don't like her. I... I need someone there to make sure. If I leave the cats, I'll need someone to take care of them. But I really need someone there full-time so that I can make sure that the cats don't bother my parakeet."

"I didn't know you had cats and a parakeet."

"Not many people do."

Miss April's words were said simply, with no explanation, and Teagan wasn't sure what to say about that. So she just nodded. She supposed it didn't matter if the whole town knew or didn't. Although, that might be one of the few things that the entire town didn't know.

"Well, I'll be happy to help. But I couldn't be there all the time."

"I know. You have farmers markets to go to and also the baking that you do. And I wasn't sure how much you helped out on the ranch, but it's not like someone has to be there constantly. But it's not too often that the house is completely empty for long stretches of time." She eyed Teagan. "Would you be able to stay all night?"

Teagan shrugged, figuring that she really couldn't say no. It wasn't like it would be a real hardship. Her sisters were on the ranch, and they could take care of everything there as long as she was back during the day to do her work. They wouldn't mind at all. As long as she continued to come and do the baking and help out wherever they needed it.

"I should be able to. When are you planning to go?"

"We leave Sunday."

Teagan blinked. She hadn't heard a word about this. She assumed that it was something that they had just decided upon, and they'd be going…she didn't know, next year? "Tomorrow?"

"Yes. We talked to our travel agent, and apparently there was a cancellation, and we got a huge discount. Just one of those things where the timing worked out perfectly." Miss April looked serene and completely innocent.

Teagan wasn't sure why the timing was such an important issue in her mind. Maybe because she found the idea that they were taking a trip to Italy in two days completely unbelievable. Who waited until the day before a big trip to find a pet sitter?

But Miss April would never steer her wrong. And Miss Helen and Miss June were both nodding serenely, neither seeming to see anything wrong with a trip like that on such short notice.

"Wow, so, that's pretty soon. Do you want me to go over right now so you can show me the cats and their food and the parakeet and its food, and everything I need to do?"

"No!" Miss April said, sounding panicked.

Teagan had started to stand from her chair. If she was going to do it, she figured she might as well get started, especially since Miss April was leaving the day after tomorrow.

She froze.

"I mean, of course we could do it right now, but I actually was hoping to get this apron finished before we left. It's a birthday gift for...my niece in...Texas, and...I wanted to mail it before I leave for Italy."

There was something off about her explanation. Something that didn't quite add up, but Teagan wasn't sure what it was. Or maybe, Miss April wasn't quite as serene as she looked, and packing for such a short-notice vacation was stressing her out more than she thought.

"If you're going to go to Italy on such short notice, maybe you should let the apron go and just focus on the essentials for now."

That was advice she heard a lot. That when things got overwhelming, just focus on the next thing that needed to be done, letting extraneous things that were not necessary fall by the wayside.

"Excellent advice. However, I sew to relax, and I think I need to continue to relax just a little bit more today." Miss April had regained her composure, and she gave Teagan another serene smile. "Would tomorrow after church work for you?"

Usually Saturdays and Sundays she spent most of the days hanging out with Deuce, but she nodded. "Sounds good." He wouldn't mind at all going with her to see what all Miss April wanted them to do.

Her. What Miss April wanted *her* to do. There she was dragging Deuce in with her, and he wasn't a part of it at all. Although, Miss April knew that pretty much anything she did, Deuce did with her. And again, Deuce wouldn't mind. He liked cats. Not as much as horses, or dogs, or cattle, or donkeys, pigs, hedgehogs, and possibly snakes. But he liked them. She was pretty sure of it.

They chatted for a bit more before Teagan left, figuring she would take care of everything she needed to back on the farm before she checked in with Deuce to see if he needed her to help him with his horses.

Staying at Miss April's house wouldn't be a hardship. She'd never stayed in town before, so it might be interesting and fun. Certainly she didn't mind looking after two cute kitties and a parakeet.

Because of their cooking and baking business, they couldn't have animals in the house, so she and her sisters didn't have any pets at all.

She left, smiling to herself, thinking about how much fun it was going to be.

Chapter 4

"Why don't you see if Deuce wants to go to the diner and take Jane's cooking class? It should only be an hour, and that should be more than enough time for me to show Teagan what she needs to do while we're gone." Miss April patted Edgar's hand, and they smiled at each other.

"That's fine. I can do that. I'll come and get you when we're done then we can head out."

"That sounds perfect." She smiled again at her husband before he walked off.

She wasn't exactly trying to get away from him, but as soon as he turned his back, she yanked her phone out of her pocket. She pulled up June's number and pressed the call button with shaking fingers.

She saw Teagan coming toward her, and she ducked behind a group of men talking about the price of wheat and whether it would be up or down this year. There was a lot of weather talk mixed in with the talk of wheat, but April wasn't paying attention. She needed to stay away from Teagan. At least until she talked to June.

"Hello?"

"June," she said, her voice hushed. "Did you ever get the cats dropped off at my house?"

"I'm sorry. I couldn't find one of my cats today. He's really shy and—"

"Okay. That's fine. But did you get them?"

"I'm getting them now. I just found the one. I'll have him at your house in...ten minutes. Just give me that much time."

"Hurry. I can't hold for long. She thinks they're mine and won't understand why I'm not rushing home. Oh! Don't forget the litter box and food and whatever else it is the cats need." She had never had cats before, and she had no idea what kind of paraphernalia they came with. A cat bed? She wasn't sure.

Hopefully, Miss Helen had already delivered the parakeet.

"Miss April?"

April straightened so fast she bumped into the shoulder of the man she had been trying to duck behind.

"There you are. I've been looking everywhere for you." Teagan touched Miss April's arm, looking concerned.

Miss April dropped her phone in her purse and tried to act casual. "Oh. I wondered what you were doing looking under the radiator. I...don't typically hang out there on Sundays. Wednesday nights are when I curl up and squeeze under it."

Teagan's eyes twinkled, but April groaned inside.

She'd already been suspicious, and she hadn't even gotten to the part where she actually had to start convincing Teagan that what she saw was what was actually happening.

She wasn't going to lie about the cats, and if Teagan came right out and asked her if they were hers, of course she would say no.

But they were at her house, and they needed to be watched. And she truly didn't know whether they would eat the parakeet or not, so that had to be watched as well.

She knew it wasn't okay to make the ends justify the means, but she felt like she was in good shape. No lying involved.

Not unless June showed up at the same time she did with cat carriers in hand.

"Hey, Miss April. Is it okay if I tag along?" Deuce asked from over Teagan's shoulder.

"About that," April said, in what she hoped was a calm, rational voice. "You know how Miss Jane has cooking classes after church on Sundays?"

"I heard about it. But I can't cook, so I figured there was no point in going."

"Deuce. That's the point of cooking classes. For people who can't cook." Teagan rolled her eyes.

"Right. Well, I figured they weren't for the people who need to learn how to turn the stove on or something."

"You're kidding. You've helped me bake plenty of times. You know how to turn the stove on."

Deuce raised his brows, as though inviting her to think about it.

April held her breath as Teagan's face scrunched up.

"I guess I do usually have you making the easy stuff."

"Sometimes I turn the oven on for you, and every once in a while, I reach in. Although once it felt like the heat fried my eyeballs when I opened the oven door, when a big blast blew up in my face. You neglected to mention to me that you need to keep your face out of the way with the first blast of hot air that comes out of the oven."

"I know. That was on me. And I'm sorry. I guess I just didn't think about it, because I've been doing it for so long."

"Well, I haven't."

"All the more reason for you to go. You'll have something good to feed me, and you can teach me this evening."

"I feel like you're trying to get rid of me."

"I'm just trying to make you into a more rounded person. A man who can work with horses, who can make pie dough, and who..." She tilted her head. "Is there anything else that you can do?"

"You are hilarious," Deuce said, keeping a straight face, before he broke into a smile.

"Right. If you can do all of the things you're already good at, and cook, it will make you more appealing to all of the female population."

"Maybe I'm not trying to be appealing to the entire female population."

"Of course not. Just to that special someone who is going to be your lifetime love whenever you get around to finding her." Teagan wiggled her brows like she was joking.

April didn't even have to try to stifle a laugh. Teagan had no idea what she was saying. If Deuce truly did find someone, surely Teagan didn't think that their relationship was going to remain unchanged? They were way too close for any woman to be comfortable with her husband having such a casual friendship with a member of the opposite sex.

"Maybe it's her that needs to get around to finding me." Deuce didn't seem the slightest bit perturbed at Teagan's teasing. In fact, he gave it right back. "And I don't see you chasing after your lifetime love. Maybe you should get a move on. Sprinting isn't your thing."

"Running at all isn't my thing. But he's going to have to catch me. I'm too busy to go running after guys."

"I thought you said busy, but I think you meant slow."

"Being slow could have its advantages. That dude, whoever he is, would catch me easier."

"Maybe you're the one who needs the cooking lessons, because apparently, no one is chasing you."

"Now, kids," April said, stepping between them. She was tempted to let them go on, not only because she had to kill some time to give June a chance to get the cats to her house, but because they were so cute together. But she didn't want them to get off the subject of cooking. She wanted Deuce to take the cooking lessons. It would be easier to juggle things if she just had Teagan. If she had both of them, they might notice that there was something in her house that wasn't conducive to a cat owner, although April had no idea what that might be.

One person was less likely to notice it than two.

"I think Teagan has a great idea. Cooking lessons would be a fun way to spend the afternoon."

Deuce raised his brows, as though his idea of fun and her idea of fun were two different things. But he didn't say anything.

"It will be entertaining, if nothing else," Teagan said with a smirk.

"I kind of thought watching you mediate an argument between two cats and a parakeet would be entertaining. In fact, that might be more entertainment than I can stand."

"Don't worry about it." She glanced at April before she looked back at Deuce. "I have the pet store on speed dial, and they're holding a parakeet for me, just in case I'm a failure at the mediation business."

April was tempted to snort laugh, but it was supposed to be her parakeet they were talking about, and she supposed she should be upset. "If this is going to be too much responsibility for you...?" She didn't want to give Teagan an out. She didn't want her to have an excuse not to catsit. That would ruin everything. Although, they'd just have to come up with something else.

"It is a lot of responsibility for her. She's not used to dealing with things that are alive. Other than me, and I learned to fend for myself a long time ago," Deuce threw right back at her.

"I heard you were coming to cooking class today."

Their conversation was interrupted by an elderly gentleman who put his hand on Deuce's forearm.

"I seem to be getting pushed in that direction, anyway. It seems kind of pointless, since I can't cook. I can't even turn the stove on. I don't want to hold the class back."

"It's okay. We'll hold your hand, walk you through everything. You won't feel a thing. Unless of course you try to touch a hot pan without a hot pad, and then you're going to be feeling a lot. So just remember, hot pads."

"And I can tell you exactly how he learned that." Mr. Blaze came up, taking Deuce's other arm. Together, with Deuce in between the two older men, they steered him out of the church.

"Cooking class is going to be good for him," Teagan said. "I'm glad you suggested it. As his sisters get older, and his parents get more involved in business, he's been alone more."

"You take care of him. But it won't hurt for him to be able to make a meal or two for the two of you."

Teagan tilted her head a little, almost as though she hadn't realized how much the two of them ate together, and the way April said it, it kind of made it sound like they were *together* together. But Teagan didn't say anything, and April, giving an inconspicuous glance at her watch and seeing that fifteen minutes had gone by and the church was almost empty, said, "Are you ready to mosey on down to my house?"

"Sure. Where's Edgar?"

"I sent him to the cooking class too. Maybe Deuce can keep him company, and they'll have two beginners instead of just one."

"You better be careful. I've heard rumors that the men are starting a TikTok channel, and they might rope Edgar into it."

"I don't think so. That would ruin their channel name, which is Three Old Coots and a Lady. If Edgar were there, it would have to be Four Old Coots and a Lady. That just doesn't quite have the same ring."

"I suppose you're right."

They started out of the church and down the steps. April's house was just a block or so down from the church, so she suggested they walk since it was such a beautiful day.

"Tell me about your cats. Are they friendly?"

April tried not to gasp. She hadn't considered that she might have to talk about the cats. She'd never even met them. She had no idea what color they were, let alone what their personalities were.

She stumbled, and Teagan put a hand on her arm.

"Are you okay?"

"Oh yes. I'm fine." April gave her a reassuring smile. "I think there is a crack in the sidewalk or something there."

Teagan looked back, her brows drew together. "Um, there isn't, but sometimes I trip over my own two feet. It's not a big deal."

"Wait until you get old. You'll do it more and more as the years go by."

Thankful they'd gotten off the subject of the cats, April searched her brain for something to talk about.

"Are you and your sisters having a booth for the summer festival?" She tried to feign casual interest and not desperation to change the subject.

"We are. Zaylee has been growing a bunch of things that she started in the house earlier this spring. She's going to have a ton of vegetables for sale, and I've been working on some new recipes."

"Sounds good."

They discussed the summer festival a little more, with April making sure to keep the subject well away from anything that had to do with cats.

It felt like a million years later that they arrived at her house. Although, April had almost stepped on the front step when she realized that Miss June's car was parked on the other side of the street.

That meant—she looked around—Miss June must still be in the house, since she was not in the car or on the street.

"Would you like to sit on the swing for a bit?" she asked, trying to sound like that was a reasonable request.

"Are you tired?"

"No, I just thought—"

Why had she said she wasn't tired? That would have been a perfect excuse. Her brain was just not working today.

"Oh, I wanted to give you a key." She pulled the spare out of her purse. It wasn't killing much time, but gave them a few seconds.

"Thank you," Teagan said as she took the key. "I'll take good care of it."

When she didn't say anything, Teagan said, "If you don't mind, I'd like to see about the cats first. Then if we have time, maybe we can sit on the swing for a bit until the cooking lessons are over."

April couldn't think of anything to say that would keep Teagan from pulling open the door.

She nodded weakly, and then as Teagan opened the door, she said, in the very loudest voice she could possibly speak in without shouting, "Did I tell you about my trip to Italy? And all the wonderful things we have planned?"

She hoped Miss June could hear her, take the hint, and hide somewhere.

"Yes. We talked about it, although you didn't give me your whole itinerary. I thought maybe you didn't have it since you scheduled it so fast."

"Oh, we have it. And I'm really looking forward to the villa where we're going to spend almost a week, just relaxing and enjoying the countryside."

"That sounds nice," Teagan said, allowing Miss April to walk in ahead of her. Thankfully.

And April gave another sigh of relief mixed with gratitude when she saw that June was nowhere in sight.

She kept talking, just in case June didn't hear them. She wasn't sure how she was going to explain it if Teagan saw June in her house. Particularly if she had a cat carrier in her hand.

She had no sooner thought that than movement under the table caught her eye. First, she thought it was one of the cats, then she realized upon a closer look that it was June.

She took one step forward, pivoted, and stood in front of Teagan, blocking her view of under the table.

Grateful that June had managed to get out of sight but wishing that she had managed to get out of sight in a different room, April decided her best bet was to get through the information Teagan needed to know as quickly as possible and get her back out of the house.

She almost jumped out of her skin as something touched her leg.

"Oh!" She cleared her throat and looked down. "This is...one of my kitties."

"He's adorable. What pretty coloring. What's his name?"

"His name?" April realized her statement was more a question. "Her name. It's...Elizabeth." Silently she apologized to her late grandmother for taking her name and putting it on a cat.

"Wow. What a nice name. What made you name him that?"

"It's a family name."

"Oh nice," Teagan said. "It's a boy, so I thought that was a little odd. But if it's a family name..."

Somehow Teagan managed to say that with a straight face and continue to stroke the cat, while April was wondering why she hadn't anticipated this situation. At least Teagan hadn't picked up on her use of "her" in regards to the cat. Surely she was expected to know the genders of her own cats.

"Where's the other kitty?"

"Oh. I...don't know." Hadn't June said one of them was shy? That was as good an explanation as any. "Sometimes he doesn't come out right away. He's a bit shy." April didn't know anything about cats at all, having never had a pet of any kind in her life before.

She supposed that she should have guessed that cats were just like kids. Whatever you said about them, they seemed to hear, understand, and deliberately set out to do the opposite just to make you look like a liar, because a second cat brushed up against her leg, and this time she really did jump.

The kitty went running.

Chapter 5

"Oh! We scared him," Teagan said, walking into the kitchen where the kitty had run to.

"Yeah. That happens," April said.

"I think he went behind the garbage can." Teagan bent over, holding the other cat. "What's his name, I'll call him out?"

"Oh. Yes. Well, he doesn't usually come to his name."

"He doesn't?"

"No. Not usually." April was not going to give any more absolutes.

"What is it?" Teagan asked again.

"Cordilia," April said, deciding to stick with female names regardless of the gender of the cat. She should have asked a lot more questions of June before she brought her cats over. Like what their names were.

Teagan didn't comment on the name but scrunched down, talking to the kitty, "Kitty, Cordelia. Look, I have your brother, Elizabeth."

The cat stayed behind the garbage can.

Teagan tried several more times while April looked surreptitiously around.

Where had June put the food? And the bowls? And the litter box?

"Well, maybe he'll warm up to me after I've been here for a little bit," Teagan said, still cuddling Elizabeth in her arms.

"Maybe," April said, not liking how weak the words sounded. She felt like she was starting to panic, because she couldn't find anything that she was supposed to be showing Teagan.

And sure enough, Teagan said, "Do you want to go ahead and show me where everything is? And tell me how much and how often you feed them."

"Sure." She wanted to do anything but.

"Oh! And I didn't see the parakeet. Is it somewhere else? I thought I'd see a cage somewhere."

"Yes. It's in a cage somewhere." It had better be in a cage. She hadn't considered that it might not be. But honestly, she had no idea. Helen had walked into her house as she and Edgar were walking out for church this morning. And April hadn't thought to tell her where to put it.

She started walking cautiously. "If we walk slowly and casually, maybe Cordilia will come out from behind the garbage can."

She hoped that was a good enough excuse to walk slow. She also hoped that Teagan didn't notice that she was looking in every nook and cranny to see where June might have put the food.

Realizing she could text June, inconspicuously, of course, she said, "I've always loved the view out that window," and she pointed to the kitchen window above the sink.

While Teagan was looking, she grabbed her phone out of her pocket.

"It's nice," Teagan said, looking out the window.

Where did you put the cat food?

"That's a ...nice view of the back of your neighbor's house." Teagan's words were wobbly but very diplomatic.

Church bells started to ring, and April just about slapped her forehead. Of course June had the sound on on her phone, and that was her text coming in. Which wouldn't have been an issue if she hadn't been hiding under the dining room table.

The church bells shut off abruptly, but not before Teagan's brows drew down and she opened her mouth.

"I just love that color of beige. If I ever get my house resided, I'm definitely going to go with that color of siding," April said in a rush.

Teagan's brows were still drawn down, but now for a different reason, thankfully. "It's very close to the color that your house is already. Is it a little bit lighter?" she asked, straining her head to see if she could see the side of Miss April's house.

"Yes. Several shades lighter, and it just looks so much brighter."

"So, about the food?" Teagan said, her hand still absentmindedly stroking the cat. At least she and the cat seemed to be getting along well, even if Teagan wasn't calling him by his given name. She had to apologize to June. Her cats might not respond to their names after three weeks with Teagan calling them something else.

Her phone beeped, and she angled herself away from Teagan so she could look at it without Teagan being able to read it.

In the downstairs bathroom.

"If you just follow me, we can walk to the bathroom, where I keep their things." Hopefully all of them.

Sure enough, when they got into the bathroom, everything was right there. Thankfully. When Teagan asked again how much she fed them, April just said that she liked to try to keep cat food in their pan at all times, and if she saw that it was empty, she filled it up.

Hopefully June's cats wouldn't be excessively overweight after three weeks of eating as much as they wanted. She figured it was better for them to get too much than for them to starve to death.

She reminded herself that she needed to give June a huge thank you for entrusting her with her cats, as badly as April was bungling all of this.

She definitely needed to tell Miss Charlene that she was not cut out for matchmaking. Her head was not in the game.

"That's great. I think I can handle that. Now, you just need to show me the parakeet so I know what I need to watch out for."

"Right." The parakeet.

"Oh. What's its name?"

"Bertha," April said, using the last of her aunts' names and hoping parakeets didn't talk or at the very least that this one wouldn't say "that's not my name."

Or was it parrots that talked?

Hopefully it was parrots.

"Is that a family name as well?"

"Yes. One of my aunts." April wondered if it was a thing for people to name their pets after deceased family members. Hopefully it was, and she wasn't quite as weird as she felt.

Walking slowly through the living room, she saw no parakeet. Checking out the hall, she still didn't see one, so she started slowly up the stairs.

She prayed that it was at the top of stairs somewhere, because it would be a little awkward to explain why she had taken Teagan on a tour of the house, if there was no parakeet upstairs to see.

Then she realized that Teagan needed to see the upstairs, if she was staying.

"I'll just go ahead and show you your room while we're walking around," she said, trying to sound casual, like that was what her plan was all along.

"That's great. You can show me where I'm supposed to sleep. I meant to ask."

"That's okay. It's been a little mixed up, with…church…and all that," April said lamely, realizing that Teagan had no idea how she'd been scrambling for the last fifteen minutes.

She showed Teagan the spare bedroom, told her to make herself at home, looked around for the parakeet, and didn't see one.

Casually looking in the bathroom and not seeing a bird, she prayed that Helen had put the parakeet in her bedroom. It was the last room, otherwise, she'd be going back downstairs and searching for it again.

Thankfully, as she opened the door, there was a cage, right on her dresser, between her jewelry box and her phone charger. Right in front of the mirror.

"That's a clever place to put it. Does it like looking in the mirror at itself?" Teagan said as she walked over to the parakeet. "Hey, Bertha. How are you?"

The cat stirred in Teagan's arms and tried to jump down onto the dresser.

"Oh my. She really doesn't like the parakeet."

"Yes. I try to keep the door closed."

"Then I can just keep it closed, and I might not even have to stay?"

"Uh...the cat can open it. I mean, he seems to anyway." April cringed. She hated liars, and she was skating on thin ice herself. Tempted to throw up her hands and admit everything, she backtracked. "He actually hasn't ever opened that door, but you know how cats are," she said, with a smile that felt more like a grimace. Italy was looking better and better all the time.

"Yeah. I've heard they're pretty resourceful. At least they are on cartoons anyway," Teagan said with a grin.

"Exactly. You can never be too careful when it comes to your parakeet."

Teagan nodded, like what April had said was perfectly rational, and they walked back out of her bedroom, with April closing the door behind her, breathing a sigh of relief and a prayer in the same breath—a prayer that June would be out from underneath the table and would have slipped outside and been able to leave undetected.

Sure enough, when they went downstairs, it was easy to see under the table from their angle coming out of the living room, and June was no longer crouching there.

Although, there was something brown sitting where June had been, and April realized what it was just as Teagan said, "If you lost your purse, it looks like you left it underneath the table. Except, that doesn't really look like your purse..."

Teagan's words drifted off at the same time April's eyes landed on the purse she had set *on* the table when they walked in from church.

"Well, what do you know? Your purse is sitting on the table. Do you realize there's a purse *under* your table?" Teagan asked, bending over and picking it up with one hand, holding the cat with the other.

"Well, my goodness. That looks like June's purse. She was in my house earlier today, and she must have dropped it, or maybe one of the cats knocked it off the table." April hoped that sounded reasonable.

"Oh. Well, I could drop it off at her place if you want me to."

"You don't need to do that, I was going to go see her later anyway." And apologize for all the things she didn't know about her cats. And ask her if they were going to die if Teagan followed the instructions that she gave. If they were, or if they were even going to be a little bit uncomfortable, April would have to figure out a way to tell Teagan that she was going to change what she had told Teagan to do. She owed that much to June. Just for letting her borrow the cats in the first place.

"But if you want to, we could sit on the porch swing and drink some tea while we wait for the men to finish up."

"That sounds great. I'll help you carry things out," Teagan said, giving the cat one last pat and setting him down.

April felt her shoulders relax, and the tension drained out of her. She thought she had managed everything just fine.

Chapter 6

Deuce looked at the sign on the diner before he opened the door, the bell jingling overhead.

It said, *Cooking class at 1 PM today.*

He and the two gentlemen escorting him had run into Edgar, Miss April's husband, on the way out of the church. Edgar, the old coot, had mentioned an interest in the cooking class as well, but on their walk to the diner, he'd suddenly remembered that he needed to drive out to Ford Hansen's place and do something with the horses. Deuce had gotten caught up in horse talk for a bit, while the other gentlemen went on ahead, and he'd practically begged to go along with Edgar. Horses were far more interesting than cooking, any day. Edgar probably would have let him, but Teagan was right. And Miss April was right as well. If he could cook a little bit, it would end up being a blessing, not just to him but to Teagan as well.

Plus, for some reason she wanted him to go, and while he didn't live his life trying to make her happy, at least he didn't think he did... Actually, pretty much everything he did, he thought about Teagan and how she would feel about it.

Maybe he did, in a small way at least, make decisions based on how Teagan would feel about them. He hadn't even realized he'd been doing it.

But that was a perfectly natural thing to do with one's best friend. She probably did the exact same thing with him. Actually, he knew she did. She was always asking what he preferred, and they would make decisions together.

Friends did it all the time.

"Hey! We have new blood!" Mr. Junior, the only man with hair standing behind the counter in the back, looked up and grinned.

"I thought it was cooking class, not taste testing for mosquitoes," Deuce murmured, wondering if this was a good idea after all.

"It is. Cooking class. And you are certainly welcome. Come on back." Jane, the owner of the diner, swayed her arm wide, in a come-here motion. When she saw him hesitate, she added, "Don't be intimidated. These guys look rough, but they've got good hearts. For the most part." She grinned, looking at the men who laughed at her.

"All right, I'm going to trust you on this," Deuce said, walking slowly back, although he knew she was right.

"Hey!" Blaze said as Deuce went through the doorway. "I just had a great idea."

"You're scaring me," Marshall said.

"No. Really. We still need a lady, you know, for our TikTok channel, Three Old Coots and a Lady."

"We know. We just haven't been able to find one yet. Relax. We'll get her," Junior said, sounding anything but relaxed.

"Well, if Deuce here can learn to cook, we could put a long-haired wig on him. He's got a baby face, and he would pass as a girl if we put a little lipstick on his lips."

"First of all, people don't want to have folks who have long hair cooking their food. That's why I'm perfect for this job," Marshall said, pointing to his bald head.

"Well, I guess it's true that we don't have to worry about any hair falling in the soup from you."

"And second of all, he would make an ugly woman." He nodded, then turned toward Deuce. "No offense."

"None taken. I think that was a compliment."

"I'd certainly take it as a compliment," Junior said.

"You have to admit that was a really good idea."

"I don't think so. We want a real lady. Even if he could look like a lady." Marshall looked over at Deuce. "I don't think you could." He looked back at his buddies. "We want a real one. I mean, there's just something about a lady that will give our channel credibility."

"Why would we need credibility?" Blaze asked.

"Maybe because we're starting a cooking channel and we can't cook?" Marshall asked. It should have been a rhetorical question, but the guys actually looked like they were thinking about it.

Deuce felt like he needed to step in. "If you're starting a cooking channel, you need to know how to cook. And if you don't, you do lack credibility. Especially if your channel is called Three Old Coots and a Lady, and you don't have a lady. That's two strikes against you. If you burn something, you're out."

Jane snorted, and Deuce grinned, showing the guys there were no hard feelings. But he was right.

"Do you know of any ladies who'd want to join our channel?"

"I thought we were going to learn to cook first?"

"We can do two things at once."

"Maybe we should learn how to use TikTok, or run it, or drive it. What do you do with it anyway?"

"Do you guys have the app on your phone?"

"One of us does." Junior looked at the other two.

"I thought you were getting it," Marshall said, looking at Blaze.

"No. I'm pretty sure it was you. I was supposed to get the dating app. Which I did. I put a profile up, too, so we can attract the lady."

"You put a dating profile up on a dating app?" Deuce probably should just let the guys talk it out between themselves, but that was too rich and he couldn't let it go.

"I sure did. Junior, what did I say?"

"Well..."

"You don't need to say on my account." He didn't want to hear it. He really didn't. It was a little bit scary.

But Junior didn't hear Deuce, because he already had his phone, and had swiped a few times with his fingers, and had started reading before anyone else could talk. "…seeks…young lady who can cook. Must be good-looking and personable because of appearing on old coots' TikTok channel. Please send a sample of cooking."

Blaze beamed. "How's that?"

"That's terrible," Jane said.

"What's wrong with it? I thought it was pretty good. I'm honest, and this will get us exactly what we want." The men started arguing, but Deuce kept quiet and stayed out of it. He wasn't even sure he could articulate what was wrong with that.

Finally, when the men couldn't agree, Marshall threw up his hands. "Tell him, Deuce. He needs to write something different."

"Something about long walks on the beach?" Deuce said, still not wanting to get in the middle of the argument.

"Yeah. That'll attract a woman. Telling her he's an old coot is a strike against him."

"I didn't say I was bald."

"Women don't mind that, not if your personality is kind and considerate, and you don't just want her because she can cook and looks good," Jane said, and while she didn't sound angry, she did sound like she wanted Blaze to listen, because he was making a big mistake.

"I think I agree with that. Even though I'm not a woman and couldn't say for sure." Deuce shoved his hands in his pockets.

"So, what should I say?"

"It's not so much a matter of what you need to say, but you have to be realistic," Jane said, lifting her brows and looking at Blaze like he was a third grader and not an eighty-year-old man.

"Realistic?"

"Think about it," she said. Then her gaze swept the men. "I'm going to show you how to make today's soup. It's easy and quick, and I think you'll love it. It's a great soup for North Dakota to curl up with on a winter night."

Deuce grinned, because Jane had effectively changed the subject, but he could tell the old men were grumbling a bit, because they still didn't have a lady for their TikTok channel.

Although, if they'd been taking cooking lessons as long as Jane had been giving them, they should have a few recipes under their belt.

Jane explained that she was going to chop up some onions and cook them in butter before she put the broth on the stove and poured the rice into it.

"Could you slide to the side a bit so I can see how you turn the burner on," Deuce said, causing the men to look at him. He looked around at them. "What? I know I could do it, but I just wanted to watch her."

All three of the men had their eyebrows up, but none of them said anything.

"Using the stove can be a little intimidating. It's hot. And there's the potential to be hurt if you touch something without your hot pad." She held one up. "That's probably the biggest thing you need to remember with the stove. Use a hot pad."

"That's true. And that's an easy thing to forget. Actually I did that the last time we were here and burned all four of my fingers," Marshall said, holding up his hand, like there was still something on it for Deuce to see.

"How would Teagan feel about being our lady? She cooks," Junior said, out of the blue, maybe.

Deuce realized he was talking to him, and immediately he wanted to say no way. But he tried a more diplomatic answer. "She actually bakes. She tells me there's a difference."

"Between baking and cooking?"

"One is typically done on the stove and is for meals and regular food. Baking is more for pies and cakes and cookies and that type of thing. Often desserts," Jane clarified for him.

"Should we do a cooking channel or a baking channel?" Junior asked, looking at his buddies.

They stared back at him, and Deuce wanted to remind them that they might have a few steps they should complete before they made a decision like that.

Instead he said, "You know, when I want to know how to use new technology, I typically ask one of the teens at church. They usually know what to do."

"Jane, do you think your daughter would help us learn how to TikTok?"

Jane's expression was long-suffering. "I'm sure she would. In fact, if that's what you guys would like to do next week, or maybe we can take a couple of weeks and learn how to use the app. And that might get you a step further on your journey."

"That was a brilliant idea, Deuce. Do you have any more good ideas for us? Like where we can find a lady?"

"Sorry. I'm all out of ideas on where to find ladies. But if I think of anything, I'll let you know."

"All right, with that settled, let's get back to the soup. You have chicken, and you're going to add that to your pot after the rice is cooked. But meanwhile, while you're waiting for your rice to cook, you can whisk your lemon juice and your eggs together."

Jane droned on, and Deuce tried his best to listen.

He must not have done too bad because an hour later, Deuce walked through the diner to the door, a container of soup in his hand.

He had enough for two. The men had insisted he take more than his share, because they were going to help Jane make more for the supper rush, when the diner opened at six.

Jane had odd hours on Sundays, and he figured it was because of her cooking classes.

She wasn't charging for them, and while it probably did save her some food prep work, if he had to guess, he'd say that she was doing it out of the kindness of her heart to give the old men something to do. And to teach them to take care of themselves.

Holding the door open with one shoulder so he could walk through, he shoved his phone in his pocket while clutching the soup container with the other.

Later, he would say that was the reason why he didn't catch Teagan.

The Highlander cow that often walked around Sweet Water, that nobody claimed as their own, came barreling down the sidewalk, but it was the pig that made Deuce step over, away from the door and back against the window.

The pig went flying by, followed by the cow, at the same time it just so happened that Teagan had been walking up the sidewalk toward the diner.

Deuce was busy getting out of the way, trying not to slam back against the window and break it, but for some reason, his head turned left and he saw Teagan just as her eyes widened, and she glanced first right then left, as though trying to figure out which was the best way to run.

She reminded him a little of a deer in the headlights as she seemed frozen in front of the barreling cow.

Thankfully, the cow went right, and Teagan did too, although for some reason, she threw herself forward, almost as though she saw him and thought she could throw herself at him and he would catch her.

But again, he blamed the fact that one hand was still behind him shoving his phone in his pocket, and the other clutching the soup, which his brain was still telling his hand that it was imperative that he not spill since he planned to share with his best friend.

Except, in less than a second, his best friend sprawled at his feet while the dust from the charging animals settled around them.

"Man, are you okay?"

She pushed herself up, laughing a little. "I've always known you're not a 'rescue the damsel in distress' kind of guy, but I feel like I just proved it, just in case there was a part of myself that was doubting it."

Deuce knew she didn't mean that as a true insult, but a part of him was offended. "I would have caught you if I could."

"I'm sure you would have," she said, dusting herself off, then turning around, her hands on her hips and looking at the retreating animals as they disappeared behind the front corner of the bakery.

She laughed again, shaking her head, and turned back around. "It's okay. I'm fine, although it was a little embarrassing." She glanced around at the mostly deserted street. "At least there was no one watching."

Deuce grimaced, because he was pretty sure the old men still in the diner along with Jane all saw Teagan fall, and they also saw him not catch her. Not that he would have been able to, even if his hands had been empty, but he figured they would be teasing him for a while about his lack, the same way Teagan would.

"Actually, looks like you have a brush burn on your palm." When she brushed her jeans off, her one hand had been a little lighter than the other on her leg, which he probably wouldn't have noticed if he hadn't been looking for it, feeling bad because he considered it his fault that she was hurt at all.

Not that the animals were his, but that she had thrown herself at him thinking he would do something, and he hadn't.

"Yeah, I guess it is. I didn't even feel it until you said something." She sighed. "Now it burns."

"Sorry. But I have comfort food." He held up the soup. "And Miss April's house is right down the road. We can go on down there, I'll fix up your hands, and we can eat some soup. It smells really good."

"Jane's been trying some new recipes, and I've been really impressed. I'm sure this is excellent as well," Teagan said, falling into step with him.

That was one of the things he loved about Teagan. She didn't hold things against people. She didn't get upset about stuff, either. Even if she truly thought he should have caught her, she wouldn't be angry about it for the next three weeks, like some girls he knew.

Like his sisters when they were younger.

They started walking toward Miss April's house. It was only a block or so away.

"That was a nice non-catch." Sam, the meter guy, smirked as they passed him.

They didn't stop, and Deuce just nodded an acknowledgment of his words.

"Where was he?"

Teagan shrugged her shoulders but didn't have a chance to say anything because elderly sisters, Francine and Betsy, walked out of the small library that Rosalin had open on a sporadic basis.

"If he were a real friend, he would have caught you." Francine shook her head, like she was giving Teagan a warning.

"Dropping you is something you expect the husband to do, not a boyfriend," Betsy added.

"Oh!" Teagan said immediately. "He's not my boyfriend."

"That's what you say. But you be careful. If a container of soup is more important than the girl he's with now, it's not going to get any better once you get married."

"We're not getting married," Teagan reiterated.

Deuce kept his mouth closed. He wasn't sure how he had become the bad guy in all of this, but apparently the townspeople expected him to be Superman and able to move at the speed of light.

Expected him to move at the speed of light and also managed to be invisible until they were ready to give him a hard time. At least that's what he thought, after the fourth person had passed him, saying something about him being clumsy and dropping Teagan, and that maybe he should consider that people were more important than soup.

By the time they reached Miss April's house, he had begun doubting himself. Maybe he should have caught her. With his hand on the door, the soup container in one hand, and Teagan waiting for him to open the door, he said, "Are you angry at me?"

Teagan blinked, her eyes shooting up to his and widening. "No! Why would I be angry?"

"Because I didn't catch you."

"I didn't expect you to. That only happens in romance novels. Where the hero manages to move the six feet that separates him from the heroine and in some miraculous way keep her from falling on the ground by twisting and putting his body under hers and blah blah blah and all of that. Life isn't a romance novel."

"I guess I'll have to take your word for that. Since I've never read one." But that was just technicalities. "Thank you. I don't understand why the rest of the town seems to expect it."

She rolled her eyes and looked down at the door with her brows raised.

He could take a hint, at least sometimes he could, and he opened it, allowing her to walk in first.

Chapter 7

"They expected you to catch me, because they think we're a couple." Teagan huffed out a breath. "I don't understand why. Since we've always been clear. And it's not like people see us doing anything other than friend things."

"I guess it's a good thing I didn't catch you, then." If that was the way things were going, they didn't want to give the wrong impression.

"Hey there," a man's voice said, causing them both to turn and look back at the porch steps.

"Hello," Teagan said, stepping forward a little, her head tilted.

"Hey, I'm Gerald from next door." He smiled, nodding toward the house right beside Miss April's.

"I'm Teagan. I'm housesitting for Miss April." She held her hand out, which Gerald grasped. "She mentioned she had a new neighbor."

"Yeah. I just moved in a couple of weeks ago. Haven't had a chance to get introduced around town."

"That's really not necessary. Everybody probably knows your name by now anyway. I'm Deuce, welcome to Sweet Water."

Gerald seemed to hold onto Teagan's hand a little longer than necessary, or maybe that was just his imagination. He wanted her to snatch it back.

But Gerald smiled a friendly smile and grabbed Deuce's hand.

"Are you and her—" He let the sentence dangle.

"We're friends," Deuce said, not really answering the question. He didn't like the way Gerald was looking at Teagan, and especially since Teagan would be staying right beside him for several weeks.

"I see," Gerald said, nodding and smiling a little bigger.

"I hate to rush away from you, but Teagan fell and scraped her hand. I'd like to go get it taken care of. I'm sure it's burning right now." Deuce opened the door wider and hoped Teagan got the hint.

"Yeah, I saw you and I figured when you let her fall on the ground you two were either married or not together." Gerald laughed like that was funny.

Deuce figured he probably would have laughed if it had been a friend saying it. But there was just something about Gerald he didn't care for. Not something underhanded or dangerous, just…he couldn't quite put his finger on it.

"I'm sure we'll see each other around," Teagan said from inside the house, and Deuce nodded as he walked in after her.

Gerald lifted a hand up and waved, and Deuce saluted him with his soup container.

He didn't watch to see Gerald turn around and leave, but shut the door behind him immediately.

He was using Teagan's hand a little bit as an excuse, but she really was bleeding, and it was the kind of scrape that really burned.

"Sorry if you wanted to stand there and talk to him," he said immediately when the door was closed.

"I didn't particularly, but I wanted to be friendly with Miss April's neighbor." She laughed. "But not too friendly. He does seem a little like he didn't want to leave."

"Yeah." He thought about asking Teagan if she felt like he was a little off. He didn't usually get that kind of feeling about people, and it was really odd that he would feel something and she wouldn't, so maybe she just wasn't saying anything.

"I probably ought to make him a casserole since he just moved in," Teagan said, rather absentmindedly as she walked to the kitchen looking at her hand.

"Sit down in the chair. I'll get some antibiotic ointment and a bandage for it."

"I don't need a bandage."

"Just for a little bit, to keep dirt from getting into it until it's done bleeding and scabs over."

She didn't argue anymore, and he figured at the very least, she'd let him bandage it up and then take it off after he left.

"Do you think Miss April will mind if I rummage through cupboards looking for a first aid kit?" he asked after he set the soup down on the table.

"She told me to make myself at home. But if we use a bunch of stuff, I'll replace it."

"If she even has one," he murmured, after looking on the refrigerator and not seeing it.

He hated to just start opening cupboards. It felt nosy, but he knew a little attention would make her hand feel a lot better.

He found a kit after he opened three cupboards. "Got it."

"This soup smells amazing," Teagan said in response.

He turned around, first aid kit in his hand, and realized she had the lid off the soup and was holding her nose over the steam.

"We'll have some, just as soon as I get your hand fixed up. Will your stomach last that long?"

"I suppose it will, if you hurry." She grinned at him, and he grinned back. And a little part of him wondered if there wasn't something to what everyone said—maybe there should be more between them.

"There's not too much that gets between you and your food."

"I know. Do it at your own risk." She smirked.

"I'm not afraid of you. I'll just drop you again."

"Ha! If you want to drop me, you have to catch me first."

"I'll keep that in mind. I'm not sure which is more satisfying."

"Catching me. So that I don't hurt my hand, and you're not stuck patching me up."

"Usually our positions are reversed," he said, referencing all the times he'd gotten bucked off a horse or pitched against the fence, and she'd ended up taking care of him.

"That's true. I didn't think of it, but I guess you do owe me." She took a breath. "Remember, I've always been very gentle and hardly ever hurt you."

"Um... I'm pretty sure the thing you say most often when you're patching me up is 'suck it up, buttercup, if you hadn't been doing something stupid, you wouldn't have gotten hurt.'"

"I have never said that to you!" she said, her attention finally completely off the food and on his face.

"Prove it." He grinned.

"You're kidding."

"See? You can't prove it. I know I'm right."

"I think you're getting me mixed up with someone else."

"No. You're the girl I've always missed catching."

"That was the second time. I guess you're zero for two."

They shared a look as they remembered the last time he didn't catch her. She was riding a horse that he had told her was dead broke, and it wasn't.

"At least it wasn't any of my animals that caused it this time anyway."

"You mean I wasn't getting bucked off of one of your horses? And you would promise me that not only would he not buck, but he would do everything I told him to do. Which, he didn't do anything I wanted him to."

"I didn't know he didn't like women. How was I supposed to know?"

"Well, I'm glad I could help you find out," she deadpanned.

"Yeah. Well, if I had been expecting him to buck, I might have been able to catch you when you fell off."

"You weren't even trying to catch me. You were worried your horse was going to run away."

That was true. And he couldn't deny it. He'd seen her fall, knew she didn't hit that hard, and had focused on catching the horse before it ended up in the next county.

"The horse wasn't bucking that bad."

"Not for you, since you're used to it. That's the first horse I've ever been on that actually bucked while I was riding it."

"Considering that you have a best friend who trains horses for a living, you're sadly lacking in your equestrian abilities."

By this time, he had dabbed the antibacterial ointment on her hand and was rooting around in the first aid kit for a bandage that would fit over the scrape and hopefully stay on.

"How soon are you going to feed me again?" she asked, watching as he dug.

"Just as soon as I'm finished. I promise, you're not going to starve to death before you get to eat the soup."

"You did get the recipe, didn't you?"

"I did, but if you want it, it's gonna cost you."

"I could say that to you the next time you come to me with a gash on your head, bleeding profusely, and want me to patch you up so you don't have to go to the ER."

"Fair enough. As soon as I'm done here, I'll text it to you." He focused on getting the bandage out of the package, placing it over her cut carefully.

"How's that?" he asked after taping down the ends.

"As long as it doesn't keep me from holding a spoon, I think it's good."

He smiled at her, thinking to himself that he appreciated the fact that she wasn't overly dramatic. That she could laugh and not get caught up in everyday life drama. That she could smile and have a good time, even when she was bleeding.

That was the kind of wife he wanted. Someone that he could take care of, who would let him take care of her and would laugh while he was doing it.

"I think it's still pretty hot. Let me pour it into bowls, and if you need it warmed up, we'll stick it in the microwave."

"You know I'm not picky," she said casually, gathering up the garbage with her good hand while he straightened up the first aid kit before closing it and putting it back in the cupboard.

He had just turned around when he felt his phone buzzing in his pocket.

Pulling it out, he looked at the screen. "It's my sister, Aspen."

Teagan nodded, grabbing two spoons out of the drawer and going over to the table to divide the soup.

"Hello?" he said, not panicking but knowing it was odd for her to call him on a Sunday afternoon.

His parents owned a wholesale construction material supply business, where they got deliveries in and sold them to contractors. They would never be millionaires, but they made enough to support the family and farm, and all of his sisters and himself were involved in the business.

He did more of the IT work at night and worked on the farm during the day, while his sisters worked in the office and in the warehouse.

"Deuce. I suppose I thought you were at Teagan's house, but I'm here and she's not, and neither are you."

"That's because she's housesitting for Miss April in town. What's up?"

"I have Minnie, and I was hoping that you or Teagan would watch her for me. I need to run in to the warehouse. I guess Dad told someone that I would grab a generator for them, and I didn't unpack them on Friday when they arrived. He wants me to do it now."

"That's fine. Can you swing by here on your way through, and you can drop Minnie off? If you'd like, I'll keep Toni for you too."

"Toni's with her friends in town. Jane is keeping an eye on them."

That was news to him. He hadn't seen the girls while he was doing the cooking lesson, but that didn't mean they weren't in the apartment behind the diner or outside. Sweet Water was a safe town for parents to allow their kids to play with minimal adult supervision.

"All right. If you change your mind about that, let me know. I'll round her up."

"All right. She has her phone, so you can text her if you want to, but I know Jane will get a hold of me if there are any problems."

"Sounds good," he said.

They hung up, with Deuce taking a minute to send the recipe to Teagan before he put his phone down.

"Minnie?" Teagan asked as she finished filling up the second bowl of soup and set the empty container down.

"Yeah. I figured you wouldn't mind if Aspen dropped her off."

"Not at all. Her dad is having trouble again?"

"I didn't ask, but I assume that his wife was supposed to take her and didn't. And he's probably working second shift at the warehouse."

That happened pretty often. Minnie's dad was a contractor who got a lot of his supplies from their company. Back when Minnie's parents were together, they knew her mom rather well, since she picked up a lot of the things they needed.

Since they had split, she had found a new job, but it required traveling. She often just didn't show when it was her turn to take Minnie.

His family might have her overnight and even till the end of the workday tomorrow before her dad was ready to have her back.

The loser in the whole situation was Minnie, and Deuce felt bad for her.

His family, especially his sisters, had always tried to step up, and he'd done his part as well. They all loved her since Minnie was a sweetheart.

"Is it terrible to say I'm kind of happy about that? I think she'll enjoy the cats, and she's such a sweetie. And Miss April has texted me and said it was okay."

"She is. I feel bad for her, but you're right. She'll enjoy the cats, wherever they are."

"They do seem to be rather shy. But maybe that's just because they don't know us," Teagan said, looking around.

"We did come in fast, with me wanting to get your hand bandaged up."

"Maybe they'll smell the soup and come out."

"I suppose that's possible." He preferred horses to cats, but animals and kids were his weakness, and he certainly wouldn't mind spending an evening playing with Minnie and petting some kitties.

Normally it wouldn't even occur to him to ask Teagan if she minded if they stayed, but maybe it was seeing the neighbor, or maybe it was the fact that people had accused them of being a pair, when they weren't, that made him think that maybe he should.

"You mind if we spend the afternoon with you?"

"Of course not," she said, her tone saying that she had no clue why he'd even asked that.

He shrugged his shoulders, responding more to her look and tone than to her actual words.

"Actually, Minnie would probably love to go for a horse ride, and it's such a nice day."

"If you want to go for a horse ride, just say so." He smirked at her, and she laughed.

"I want to go for a horse ride, but I do think Minnie would enjoy one too, and we should take her."

He had that feeling again as Teagan looked up at him. That feeling that it didn't matter what she asked, he would do it.

He'd always thought that was a friend feeling, but maybe talking to the ladies today, the ones who asked when they were finally going to get together, had made him wonder if that's what it truly was. Or if he was just lying to himself.

Chapter 8

Deuce pulled in front of his house. He'd texted his sister to let her know he'd meet her there instead so that they could go horseback riding with Minnie.

He realized he hadn't thought of it very often until the last few days, but it wasn't every person who had a best friend who was willing to do anything with him. Including picking up someone else's kid and watching her for an afternoon.

"I guess I don't say this very often," he started out, stumbling a little, because they were unfamiliar words. "But...thank you. I appreciate the fact that you roll with whatever happens and hang out with me even though it's kind of lame to spend the afternoon with a little girl."

"You know I don't mind," Teagan said cheerfully, as though she didn't hear the emotion in his voice. Maybe she didn't want to.

"No. I'm serious. I appreciate you."

She stopped, her hand on the latch, looking across the seat at him.

"Are you okay?" Lines appeared between her brows. She tilted her head a little, and he grinned.

"Stop it."

"Stop what?"

"Stop using that sixth sense thing you have on me."

"You're the one who was getting all emotional."

"You're cheating."

"I'm not cheating when I just use what I have."

"I don't like it when you read my mind."

"I don't read your mind. You know that. I just... I don't think of paying attention, deep attention, to you. And maybe that's what you were just saying. I take advantage of you as much as you were thinking you might take advantage of me." She shook her head as though shaking off that thought. "I didn't think you were taking advantage of me. I don't agree with that. We just...work together. You know, like you stop and explore an old, abandoned house with me for a bit, and I hang out with you and help you with your horses."

"I know, but isn't that what people do? They just assume that their friends are down for what they've always been down for, and sometimes we bump along without actually talking to each other."

"Communication?" she asked, a knowing grin on her face. One that teased him a little.

"We don't have that kind of relationship," he said quickly, just because everybody always seemed to be pushing them into it. And he didn't want her to think that he was getting on that bandwagon.

Although...was he?

That was a thought he didn't want to entertain.

"I know. And I know you don't think so either." Her face got serious for once. "Even if the rest of the town seems to think..."

"They don't understand us the way we understand us," he said, trying to fill in the words that she didn't seem to be able to find. To make things easy again. Why had he tried to disturb their casual relationship by getting emotional?

That wasn't supposed to be him, anyway. It was supposed to be her.

It was supposed to be the woman who got all emotional and thought that they needed to communicate more. And who got thankful and appreciative and all the things that he had been feeling, and that really made him uncomfortable.

Except, Teagan felt like more than a best friend to him. Not in an attractive he wanted to marry her today kind of way. Not really. But...just someone that he didn't want to lose.

"Have you ever thought about what life would be like if we didn't have each other?"

There he was again. Asking crazy questions. Why?

Someone must have said something that jarred something inside of him. Because he didn't usually think about losing Teagan. He didn't think about Teagan at all. She was just there.

Slowly her hand dropped from the door latch, and she turned to face him more fully.

"That's deep," she said slowly.

"I'm sorry. I'm not sure what's wrong with me." That was the truth. He could always tell Teagan the truth. That was the one thing about their relationship. They laughed a lot, and they had a great time together, but he could always tell her the truth, even if it was inconvenient.

"So there is something wrong?" she asked, still talking slowly.

"I don't know. I just... I don't usually get all serious and emotional, but... I'm feeling odd."

"Well, they're gonna wonder why we're sitting here in the pickup, and that's going to give people even more reason to talk. Let's get Minnie, we'll saddle a couple of horses, and chances are, Minnie will fall asleep against you like she usually does, and we can try to figure out what your problem is. You know I'll help if I can."

She didn't even have to say that. He knew it. He knew she would help. She'd do anything for him, literally anything.

"All right. That sounds good. Actually, I really don't even want to talk about it anyway. I'm not sure why I brought the subject up."

"It must be something you're thinking about. Or worried about. Which you know you don't have to. I'm not going anywhere."

"No one ever thinks they're going anywhere, but they do."

"But I'm not." Her voice was firm but laced with compassion, like she was offering him comfort.

He wasn't sure whether he liked that or not. He supposed he did like the fact that she felt compassion toward him, but he didn't like feeling needy or like someone had to cater to him in order to keep him from getting emotional.

They pulled their door latches up and stepped out of the truck, slamming the doors at the exact same time.

Without saying anything, they walked around the front of the truck and walked side by side up the walk.

Aspen stood at the door holding Minnie who bounced up and down on her hip, shouting in her little girl voice, "TT! TT! Hold me!"

"She wants you," he said, pretending to be offended. After all, he was the one who was supposed to be watching her.

"You know the second I have her in my arms, she's going to want you. That's just the way kids are," Teagan said with a grin, which he returned.

Not only was it true, but he appreciated the fact that Teagan wasn't competitive with him. She wasn't trying to make Minnie like her more than she liked him, but was always looking out for him. That's just the way she was, and maybe that was another one of the things that he didn't appreciate about her like he should.

"Thanks, kid," he said, reaching a hand out and ruffling her hair, the way he knew she hated, before he opened the door and held it for her to walk through as she slapped at his hand, getting it away from her hair.

"What was the point of me combing that this morning?" she said, a tone of mock irritation in her voice as she walked by him. She didn't give him a chance to answer but said, "Hey, kiddo!" And she held her hands out to Minnie.

"TT!" Minnie said, wrapping her little arms around Teagan's neck and squeezing hard.

Teagan hugged her back and said in a slightly choked voice, "Hey, Aspen. How are you?"

"DD! DD! Let me have DD!" Minnie said, holding her arms out to Deuce.

Deuce met Teagan's eyes, with a knowing look, and could easily read that Teagan was saying *I told you so.*

He grinned in acknowledgment as he took the little girl in his arms, all warm and soft and cuddly. She wrapped her chubby arms around his neck and squeezed tight.

"I'm fine."

"Minnie and I made up a little snack box for you guys while we were waiting for you."

"Snacks!" Minnie said excitedly. "I helped." She grinned, the big grin that showed all the little teeth that she had in her mouth, and the kind of grin that made Deuce's heart melt when he looked at it.

"I hope you packed a lot, because Deuce is always hungry, and if we're going to get anything to eat, there needs to be a good bit there." Teagan tickled Minnie's belly as she giggled and nodded her head, agreeing that Deuce was indeed a hog and that she had packed a lot.

"Did you just call me a pig?"

"No. I would never..." Teagan said, her voice holding disbelief that he would even suggest such a thing.

"I think she did," he said, looking at Minnie and putting his forehead next to hers, and rubbing her nose with his.

Minnie giggled again and took both chubby hands, holding onto his face so she could rub his nose with hers.

"I know she's going to be tired. She has her giddy sleepiness going on right now."

"That's okay. She usually falls asleep when we start out. It's the motion of the horse that lures her eyes closed, I think," Deuce said.

"I am not taking a nap!" Minnie said determinedly.

"Of course not," he agreed easily. She could think that all she wanted to, but experience had borne out that she would be sleeping by the time they'd gone a mile.

"Uh-oh. What do I smell?" Deuce said, wrinkling up his nose.

"Diaper change!" Minnie said, smiling wickedly.

"It's your turn," he said, handing Minnie to Teagan, who took her reluctantly.

"Are you sure about that? I think it's yours."

"Would I lie about something like this?"

"Yes?" Teagan said.

"You know I wouldn't."

"No. I'm sure you wouldn't. But you might conveniently forget something. Which is what I think is happening here."

"Fine. If you want me to change her—"

"No. Just remember, the next time it's your turn." Teagan lifted her brows at him before looking at Aspen, as though she were the witness, and saying, "Where's her diaper bag?"

"In the living room by the chair," Aspen said easily.

"Make sure you get it all out, Minnie," Deuce called after them. "I don't want to have to change your diaper for at least a week."

"Maybe I'll only pretend to change it so that you have to change it later today."

"You wouldn't do that to that poor little girl," Deuce said, smirking, because he knew Teagan would never.

Teagan disappeared in the room. Deuce thought she turned her head and stuck her tongue out just as she was walking in, but he couldn't say for sure.

"When are you two going to get together?" Aspen said, her voice low, but it held laughter as she shook her head.

Deuce turned and looked at his sister. "Why is everybody saying that to us?"

"Maybe it's because you should get together," Aspen said, making it sound like it was obvious.

"We're friends. Why can't people get that through their thick heads?"

"Maybe people are trying to get something through your thick head," Aspen said reasonably. Her eyes softened. "Like we're always trying to get Brooklyn to see that Cormac might not necessarily be someone that she has to hate?"

"That's a completely different story. You know that's not the same thing." Deuce knew there was something between Brooklyn and Cormac that had made it impossible for them to be together.

Aspen didn't give him a chance to say anything more. "You and Teagan were made for each other. Look how well you guys get along."

"And if we did become more than friends and try to have a relationship, we could ruin everything."

"What if you don't?"

"What do you mean?"

"I mean, what if you don't become more?"

"Then we'll stay friends forever. And everything will be perfect." He believed that. If they became more, and it messed everything up, it could ruin things for the rest of their lives.

"What if someone else comes along? That's what I'm talking about. What if Teagan gets a boyfriend?"

"Then I'll be happy for her."

"Where are you going to fit into that?"

"Where I always have. I'll be her maid of honor." Not likely, but she got the idea.

"Do you really think that if Teagan gets a boyfriend, you'll just carry on as usual?"

Chapter 9

Aspen had taken Minnie's sippy cup and was rinsing it out in the sink, but she stopped, turning the water off and just standing there looking at Deuce. Willing him to think about it.

Normally he liked to just give surface answers. He didn't like to think too deeply. But Aspen was putting another piece of the puzzle together on something that had been bothering him, the same thing that probably prompted him to ask Teagan what he had when they had been sitting in the driveway.

They couldn't just be friends forever.

They were getting to the point where their lives were almost certainly going to change at some point, and if he didn't guide the direction of the change, they could end up changing in a way he didn't like.

"If I try to have anything more with Teagan, and I'm not saying I'm totally closed to that idea." He glanced toward the living room where Minnie's voice sang some kind of song of which he couldn't recognize the tune or the words. He was pretty sure Teagan couldn't hear him. "And I would not want her to know I said that. After all, there is a lot at stake."

"I agree." Aspen gave a nod, not needing to say that their friendship was special. That they had something that normal people didn't.

"And I don't want to mess that up."

"Then do it carefully. But do it."

"Do you know something I don't?"

"No." Aspen's gaze was steady. Which was a good thing, because her words had made his heart drop. If Teagan had an interest in someone, he would have thought he would be the first one she would tell, but…maybe he wouldn't be. Maybe she would be as uncomfortable as he was at the idea that their relationship might change.

"But I do know that she's pretty. Maybe not beautiful in a pinup kind of way, but sweet and kind and someone that turns people's eyes. One of these days, she might slip away from you, and I would hate to see that happen."

"Hey. I'm a catch too."

"You're my brother. That means I'm just trying to get rid of you. Marry you off to the first person who will have you." Aspen laughed, and he laughed along with her, knowing she was joking. Indeed, her next words were, "You're a catch too. I know that there have been ladies who were interested, and you let them slip by. Good ladies, ones who would have made an excellent wife and mother. I can only assume you did that because you had Teagan."

He supposed that was true. He hadn't thought about it that way. Not when he'd been fending off unwanted advances. He'd just been happy he had Teagan and not interested in women who just didn't seem to compare.

"All right. She's changed. If you want to confirm that it's a brand-new diaper, you can go ahead." Teagan came out, with Minnie on her hip. In a stage whisper, she said, "Remember what I said about pooping in your diaper as soon as we go outside."

Minnie nodded her head, like she could actually control such things at her age.

"If she has that much ability, to just turn it on and turn it off, she ought to be putting it in the potty," Aspen said, lifting one brow at Minnie, who probably had no idea what in the world she was saying but laughed anyway and then buried her head in Teagan's shoulder.

"You guys be good," Aspen said, turning the tap back on and rinsing out the sippy cup.

He and Teagan exchanged a grin as Teagan thanked Aspen, picking up the box she'd packed and following him back out the door.

Teagan held Minnie, giving her a lead rope to hold while he brushed Reba, which was the horse Teagan always rode, and Munchy, the horse he used for trail rides. Normally, if it were just him and Teagan, he would take one of the horses he was training, but since he would probably have Minnie on his lap, he wanted to take a horse that he knew would be as safe as a horse could be.

From his experience, there was no such thing as a completely safe horse. Any horse was liable to go crazy over a little bit of nothing, but Munchy was as bombproof as they came.

Plus, he was pretty. A palomino, with a golden mane and tail and a sunset-colored coat.

"Reba likes to be scratched right here," Teagan said to Minnie, showing her where Reba, his buckskin, liked to be scratched.

Minnie got enthusiastic about the scratching, but Reba didn't care. She was laid-back and easygoing, which was the exact kind of horse that Teagan needed.

For as much horse things as she'd done with him over the years, she'd never gotten comfortable on a horse's back.

Reba was not the kind of horse he'd keep around, not for any other reason other than Teagan. Just like he had Munchy for Minnie.

It didn't take long to tack up the horses and to start in the direction they always went. They'd done it so many times together that neither one of them asked the other, they just guided their horses in that direction, him with Minnie on in front of him, and Teagan riding easily beside him.

There were a few places where the trail got narrow and she would fall back, but for the most part, they, and their horses, knew the drill.

They listened to Minnie chatter while she played with Munchy's mane, telling them in sentences they couldn't quite understand how her day had gone.

Eventually, she talked less and less, as her head laid back against his chest, until she grew completely silent and limp in his arms.

Deuce kept his arms around her, feeling the weight of responsibility as she completely trusted him to take care of her.

The weight of responsibility and a stirring of butterflies in his stomach, which was almost unheard of when he was with Teagan.

He kept his mouth shut, not wanting to broach the subject that they had agreed they'd talk about later.

After what Aspen had said and what he'd been feeling, he almost felt like it was something he was supposed to talk about. Like God had prompted him to think about it.

But he didn't want to take the risk. Didn't want to consider doing anything that might drive Teagan away. Or make things awkward between them.

"Are you feeling better?" Teagan asked, her voice sounding casual as her horse plodded along beside his.

"I guess."

"You don't sound very certain."

"I suppose we're just not guaranteed tomorrow."

"And so you want to make sure you don't take advantage of your friends today?" Teagan sounded like she wasn't quite sure if they were talking about the same thing.

He wanted to latch onto that. Make that the real reason he was talking to her. Make out like that was what he wanted to say. And it was something good. Something he probably didn't think enough about.

"That's a good point. I do take advantage of you. I just assume you'll be here. And I guess maybe God's been opening my eyes to the idea that you might not be."

"But not just me. Your sisters too. I mean, anyone could go at any time."

"Not die necessarily. Although that's possible. But like I we've often said about your sister Brooklyn and Cormac. Those two have the explosive kind of relationship that, if they ever did get together, they'd probably be married the next day."

Teagan laughed, but then she sobered. "Do you know whatever happened with them?"

"I think it happened in school. But they were younger than us, and if it was a big thing in town, I never heard about it." He grinned. "I don't mean to be nosy about your sister."

"You're not. I mean, it's common knowledge that they're enemies. But I suppose whatever made them become enemies might not be so common. My guess is there was some kind of misunderstanding, and Brooklyn, who likes to be in charge and in control of things, was embarrassed."

"She doesn't embarrass easily."

"No. But when she does, it's a pretty big deal."

"I guess when you're used to being in charge, the feeling of not is not a good one."

"Yeah. But I'm just guessing. Maybe she did something to him. But she seems to be the one who really has the issue. I've talked to Cormac plenty of times over the years, and he's never had such an adverse reaction as what Brooklyn does." She paused. "Maybe he secretly likes her?"

Deuce grinned. "Ever the romantic, aren't you?"

"There's nothing wrong with that." Her voice was soft, and she kind of looked ahead, like she might be thinking about something.

Could she be thinking about someone?

Deuce had never before been afraid to ask her what she was thinking, but he wasn't sure he wanted to know if she were thinking of a man other than him.

He couldn't ask.

Instead, he said, "Do you see us being friends forever?"

His voice sounded more serious than what he wanted it to. But he couldn't take the words back.

She heard his serious tone, and her head turned, and she gave him that look, the one he didn't want her to give him. The one where she seemed to see inside of him, ferreting out all of his thoughts and feelings and being able to read the emotions that lay under his words.

He caught himself holding his breath and tried to breathe out, breathe normally, look casual.

"Are you sick?" Her eyes grew wide. "Were you at the doctor's and you didn't tell me? How could you be at the doctor's and not tell me?" She mumbled like she was talking to herself. "Surely you would tell me if you made an appointment. Surely you wouldn't have some kind of issue that you didn't talk to me about? Right?" She turned her head, almost looking angry that he might dare to keep something from her.

"I'm fine. Healthy as this horse."

She didn't even laugh at his small attempt at humor. Her eyes narrowed, almost as though she suspected his humor was an attempt to deflect her attention, and it kind of was. "So you're serious?"

He nodded. Slowly.

"You're really thinking about this, just out of the blue?"

He nodded again, looking at his horse's ears and not at his best friend.

"And you haven't been to the doctor?"

"No."

"You're not feeling sick?"

"No."

"And there's nothing wrong with you?"

"No."

"And you truly want to know where I see us going? If I think we're going to be friends all of our lives?"

"Yes."

The idea of examining their relationship. Of defining it. Of putting some kind of terms to it. It was not something that he had ever entertained. He wasn't sure it was a good idea now. But there it was. Out there between them.

"Why wouldn't we be?" She sounded truly perplexed.

"People grow. They change. You...might get a boyfriend."

"And if I do, he'll just have to understand that you're part of my life too."

"But it wouldn't be the same."

He didn't have to spell it out for her; she seemed to understand what he was talking about, and she fell silent. Maybe thinking the same things he had been thinking earlier.

"I guess that's kind of depressing to think about," she finally said as the horses started making the big loop to head home.

That wasn't exactly the direction he had hoped her thoughts had gone in, but he supposed it was a start. Maybe she just needed the seeds of knowledge planted the way he had. Because he had never thought of any of that before, and he wasn't even sure what set him off now.

"I guess I was just thinking that life changes. You know? You think things are always going to be the same. The people that you know now are always going to be around. But it doesn't work that way. Hardly ever. And I don't want to take advantage of the people who are around me. My sisters, true. But you. You're the one constant in my life. You've been with me through thick and thin, sometimes even more so than my own parents. And I go along, just assuming you're going to continue to be there. And that's not a good assumption. I... I don't like to think I've taken advantage of you, because I don't want to think I have."

"You haven't! Our relationship has been give-and-take, and that's part of the beauty of it. We don't keep track. If you need me, I'm there. And if I need you, I don't have to ask. You're standing at my elbow waiting to help. Or jumping in without me saying anything."

"Not taking advantage of you in that way. But just assuming that you'd always be there. There is no guarantee."

"Of course not. There's no guarantee for anything. Even people who made vows to each other don't always keep them. Just because you stand in front of a preacher doesn't guarantee that you're going to have the person that's standing with you for the rest of their life. They might or might not keep their word. There is no guarantee."

She echoed his words, and it was funny that she used a wedding as her example. Since that's the direction he thought he wanted to go. He was sure she didn't realize that though. Didn't realize that he had actually been thinking along those lines.

"If you know the person that you're vowing your life to, if you can count on them to keep their word, if they're a person of character and integrity, it really is a guarantee."

"People change. You have. I have too. We're not the same people we were ten years ago."

"But we've grown together. And that's the thing. When people get married, they grow together."

"Unless they grow apart."

"You can make it so that that doesn't happen."

"Can you?" She looked over at him, her head tilted, her eyes having that look that said she knew something he didn't.

He knew that look. It made him close his mouth and think a little harder. What was she saying?

Chapter 10

Finally Deuce shrugged his shoulders. "What do you mean?"

"I mean, you can't control anyone but you. The person you're married to might have faults, and you know that when you get married. You know you're not marrying someone who's perfect. And I suppose, you always hope that they work on those faults, and they get better. The same way you want to work on your faults and become a better person. But what if they don't? What if they decide that they're content with the way they are? Or, worse, what if they decide that they don't need to work on becoming a better person, and they just want to take the easiest path in life? The one of least resistance? The one that makes them feel good at the time?"

She was quiet for just a second, and he didn't say anything, because he knew she was right. "They might start out with excitement and enthusiasm and all of the things that you love, and then maybe something happens. They lose a job. They lose a child. A parent dies. Or they just get tired of life. And they decide that they'd rather live in an alternate reality, or maybe they think they work hard, and they come home and sit in front of the TV with a beer can in one hand and the remote in another. And...there is no communication. You can't control that. You don't know how someone else is going to react to life events. You don't even know how you are going to react."

There was one small flaw in her thinking, so while he could agree with the majority of it, he had to say, "If you're a Christian, if you're dedicated to becoming better, then those bumps in life should make you turn and run and try to be closer to Jesus."

"They should. But sometimes we get bitter. Sometimes we get discouraged. And I'm not saying that if someone's discouraged it's the end of the world, but sometimes we get discouraged or sad or lonely, and we look to other things to fulfill us, drugs, alcohol, mindless TV, electronics, even books give us an escape into a fantasy world, and those things take the place of Jesus for us. They give our life some weird kind of meaning and keep us from having to face the difficulties that we want to avoid. Keep us from having to grow and stretch ourselves. Keep us from having to have those hard relationships with people."

"So you're saying there's just no point? That everyone's going to self-medicate with books and TV and there's no point in trying to have a lifetime relationship?"

"No." She drew the word out, like she wasn't sure exactly what she had been saying. "You're saying there's no guarantees in life. And I'm agreeing with you. You just don't know. Even if you say vows and think you're marrying someone you know. You still have no idea how that will turn out. And that's not necessarily good or bad. I think it's just life."

"And we sometimes judge other people based on how their relationships turn out, when it's maybe not their fault?"

"Yeah. That's true. We do. Or we judge ourselves. We tell ourselves that we're a failure, when maybe it wasn't us. Although, I think that's pretty uncommon. I think most of the time, we're all too willing to blame things on someone else and not take responsibility for ourselves."

He supposed that was true and didn't really have any answers. But he did know one thing. "You can look at someone, see how they've handled things in the past, and you can have a good idea of how they're going to handle things in the future."

She nodded. He felt a small thrill of victory slide through him. She was agreeing, and maybe she could see that in him.

"So you think we're going to be friends forever?" he prodded again, and he wasn't sure why. Wasn't sure what he was hoping to get her to agree to.

Their horses plodded along while she chewed her lip, and he liked that she was giving thought to his question.

Finally, she said, "I think the odds are stacked against us. I think when I have a husband and you have a wife and we have kids and families, we're not going to have time to just take a Sunday afternoon and spend it together. No one does, even if we were the same gender, which the fact that we're not makes it even harder." She lifted her shoulder. "But I don't see any point in worrying about that now. The future will take care of itself. God knows. I think that's the key. I think that's the key to all of it. You depend on God to work things out. Because you know that whether the person that you're in a relationship with stays faithful, or whether they don't, God has it all orchestrated. And He will only allow you to go through the trials that He wants you to have. We forget that."

"That's true. I agree. I suppose, that goes along with what I was saying earlier. I don't want to take the people in my life for granted. I want to make sure that they know that I appreciate them, care for them, and they know that, not just because I say it, but because my actions say it. And that's all I can do. I have to trust God to handle the rest."

She looked over at him, nodding and smiling. "I was kind of feeling like that was a depressing conversation. I've often thought how sad it is when I see people get divorced, that they couldn't stay together. But it takes two, no matter how badly one person wants to. And that's sad. But you're right. Even if you're the one who wants to stay together, and you don't get to, you can take comfort in the fact that God knows and He's allowing it."

"And maybe He'll allow you to help people going through the same thing," Deuce added while Teagan nodded in agreement again.

He wasn't really satisfied with their conversation, but he felt like they had waded in the deep end of the pool long enough, so he said, "I was thinking about getting you a different horse. One with a little more get up and go, a little more spirit."

"No!" Teagan said in mock horror, patting Reba's neck. "Reba is my horse. We've been together forever." She was making a little fun of their earlier, heavier conversation, and he laughed along with her.

They talked along those lighter lines until they reached the barn, where there was a strange truck parked at the corral.

Two men he didn't recognize at first were leaning on the fence.

As they pulled to a stop, Minnie, who had been waking up as the horses' pace picked up as they headed toward the barn, wiggled in his arms.

"I'll take her. We'll go see the chicks under the heat lamp while you talk to these fellows."

"Thank you," he said, looking into her eyes, so she understood that he was thinking about what he had said earlier about not taking advantage of her and really meaning that he appreciated her when he was thanking her.

She grinned, knowing exactly what he was saying, as she pulled Reba to a stop and slid out of the saddle, pulling the reins down over her head and handing them to Deuce while Deuce handed Minnie to her.

He took a minute to watch Minnie snuggle into her arms, putting her childish hands around Teagan's neck, before Teagan nodded at the men who were standing at the corral and walked off.

"Nice day for a ride," one of the men said, putting the foot that had been on the first rung down on the ground and walking toward him with his hand out. "My name is Jonah. We've met before, but I wasn't sure if you remembered me."

"I do. Thanks for jogging my memory." Deuce shook the proffered hand. "You're my neighbors to the west."

"We sure are. I'm Gideon." The other man held his hand out.

"I'm glad you guys came around."

"I hope we didn't interrupt your Sunday afternoon ride?"

"No. We were done. Minnie has a short attention span, and we can often get her to relax and take a little rest, but we can seldom get her to stay asleep long. She was waking up, and it was a good thing we were headed home."

The men nodded, but they did it in such a way that it made Deuce think they weren't used to children.

"So, we bought the ranch next to you."

"Yeah. I didn't get the impression that you two were brothers though," Deuce said casually, not wanting to pry, but considering that one of the men was dark and one was light, and they didn't look anything alike, he assumed they weren't family.

Jonah grinned. "We're not. We met in the Air Force. There are six of us on the farm. Actually, five now that Smith decided he's going to stay on his aunt's farm and marry Abrielle."

"Women. They make men do the craziest things," Gideon said with a smirk.

Deuce couldn't argue with that.

"So anyway, five of us. And our business is crop dusting."

"That makes sense, since you were in the Air Force."

"Yeah. Several of us can fly. We researched it. There wasn't anyone around, and we figured we could make a go of it up here."

"You probably can. Particularly if you have a helicopter too."

"We're working on securing one. Just a small one, but powerful." Gideon looked eager at the idea, and Deuce figured he was probably one of the pilots. He just had that look in his eye. Half crazed, if

Deuce had to say, but he supposed it was just an adventurous spirit or maybe an unwillingness to be bound by gravity.

Deuce was more than happy to keep both feet on the ground. But he admired and respected men who wanted more.

"But we're also going to try to farm our own place. Everyone says in order to do that, you need a couple of good cow horses. None of us know anything about them, but your name kept coming up in conversations we had around town. So we figured we'd come out here and give you a visit. See what you had to say."

"Are you looking to buy a good cow horse? Or are you looking to learn about them?"

"Both." Jonah lifted his hat, adjusting it on his head before he continued. "We were told you were honest. And so, I feel like I can admit that we know airplanes, and there is a welder and a mechanic among us as well, but none of us have any experience in horses. We could buy a good cow horse, but I'm going to assume that there are some tricks to riding it, same way there are some tricks to flying an airplane. You don't just hop in the cockpit and take off on your first day. There's a few things you have to learn."

"That's a great analogy." Deuce laughed. He'd never heard it put quite that way before. "But I hope that horses are a little simpler than airplanes. Although, I honestly couldn't tell you, because I've never even flown in an airplane, let alone piloted one."

"We can fix that if you want to," Gideon said with a grin.

"Let me make sure you're happy with your horses before I get into an airplane with you," Deuce said, with humor in his voice. He liked the look of these guys, and he figured they would never do anything unkind.

But they laughed, the way he expected them to.

"I think that's a good idea." Gideon glanced at Jonah, and they shared a look. "I suppose the quality of his airplane ride will reflect the quality of the horse he sells us."

"I think you guys are threatening me," Deuce said easily.

"Nah. We're just making sure we're not going to get swindled."

"That's too bad. I could see you guys coming a mile away."

"That's what we thought."

They talked a bit about riding horses, and Deuce told them about the ones he had in training and the ones he thought would be best for them, and they set some times for the men to come out so Deuce could help them with their riding. He figured it wouldn't take long for them to learn the things they needed to know. Neither one of them seemed like they would be afraid or that they would get bucked off and not want to get back on. He could take their lessons pretty fast and have them on their horses by the middle of summer.

The men left, with things settled between them, and Deuce moseyed over to the chicken coop, looking for Teagan and Minnie.

It was good to know he had such good neighbors, men he could count on, even if they weren't experienced ranchers. They'd probably need some guidance for the North Dakota winter. He'd be happy to help them out. He'd be willing to bet he'd just met two men who would end up being lifelong friends.

Chapter 11

Teagan drove back to town, a smile on her face.

She'd had a great afternoon with Deuce and Minnie. The little girl could always make her smile and made her feel so loved with her big hugs and her sloppy kisses and her exuberant joy for life.

She loved the baby chicks, and they'd eventually eaten their snacks right beside the heat light so they could watch them play while they ate.

But Teagan had felt like she ought to get back home to Miss April's house. Mostly because she hadn't seen Elizabeth or Cordilia since that morning and figured she'd better make sure they were okay.

She'd feel terrible if anything happened to them.

Deuce had offered to come back with Minnie, but there wasn't much for Minnie to do at Miss April's house once she'd seen the cats, and Teagan hadn't been able to get a hold of Miss April to ask if it was okay.

She was sure Miss April wouldn't care but hated to invite a young child to her house without her approval.

Plus, she wasn't sure how the cats would respond to a toddler, considering they weren't exactly super warm to her.

She thought about that as she unlocked the door and walked in, looking around, trying to see if she could see either one of them.

Elizabeth came right away, running over like he had missed Teagan.

But there was no sign of the other one.

She shut the door and bent down, petting Elizabeth, relieved that at least one of the cats seemed to be adjusting okay to Miss April's absence.

Maybe that was why Gerald's voice startled her so much.

"Knock, knock," he said.

Teagan almost fell down as she twisted, scaring Elizabeth who ran under the couch. "My goodness. I wasn't expecting a visitor."

Had the man been sitting on his porch and she missed him? How did he know she was here?

"Mind if I come in?"

"Well, I—" She didn't get anything else out before he opened the door and stepped in.

"You've been gone most of the day," he stated, and maybe it seemed like casual conversation to him, but it seemed like prying to her. Why was he keeping tabs on what she did today? She barely knew him.

If he were a good friend, she wouldn't have given it a second thought.

"I went to church," she stated, not wanting to give a rundown of her day and realizing he hadn't really asked about it. Just stated that she was gone.

"Yeah. That's way too early for me to get up on a Sunday. It's the only day I have to sleep in."

She nodded. She'd heard that excuse plenty of times before from other people on why they didn't go to church on Sundays. It was fine. She certainly wasn't in a position to judge anyone. However, she supposed that if she ever needed God to help her, she wouldn't want Him to use the excuse that He was sleeping in and couldn't be bothered. So, she had decided that she wouldn't use that excuse to not go to church.

Of course, she didn't mention that to Gerald. And of course, she knew that that wasn't truly the way God worked. But in all of her relationships, she always tried to be the one who gave more. It was not a competition or anything, she just didn't want to be in a lopsided relationship where someone was always giving to her, and she was always taking and never offered anything in return.

If a person truly was supposed to do unto others as they would have them do unto them, then she would try to be the person that she wanted to be in a relationship with, someone who was generous with their time, generous with their possessions, loving and kind, and always willing to go above and beyond.

She was in a relationship with God, and while she could never outgive the Lord, she could certainly give him an hour on Sunday.

Still, it was a personal preference, and not one she expected Gerald to share, so she didn't say anything.

They seemed to lapse into an awkward type of silence. Gerald stuck his hands in his pockets and just looked at her, standing inside the door. As she, uncertain of what to do, definitely not wanting to invite him in, stood staring at the bottom of the couch where Elizabeth had disappeared.

Finally, when Gerald didn't seem like he was going to say anything more, she said, "I was going to take a shower, so if you don't mind..." She left the statement open ended, insinuating that he needed to leave.

He didn't take the hint.

"I don't mind. Go right ahead." He walked over and sat down on the couch.

She stared at him, her mouth just a little open, but she barely noticed and certainly didn't have the presence of mind to close it.

What in the world was she supposed to do?

Was it safe to let him sit in the living room without her supervision while she took a shower?

She didn't see anything valuable lying around, and she was pretty sure that when she had been in Miss April's bedroom to see the parakeet, there had been a desk in the corner which was probably where she kept her bills and other personal information.

Maybe if she locked the bathroom door, she would be safe taking a shower at least. Surely he wouldn't go upstairs to the bedroom and rummage around while she was right across the hall in the bathroom?

She decided she really didn't have any choice but had to take the risk.

Waiting just a few more seconds, like he'd suddenly pop up from the couch, realizing how rude he was being, and take his leave, she finally turned and left.

She took the world's fastest shower. Not because she wanted to get back out to Gerald, but because she was terrified that he was going to do something to Miss April's stuff and she would be answerable to it. She didn't want to allow anything bad to happen, not on her watch.

Even though she was only supposed to be catsitting, she assumed that Miss April was depending on her to make sure that nothing happened. Especially since Gerald was in there...because of her? It wasn't like she invited him in.

Maybe she should talk to Miss April and find out exactly how close she was with her neighbor. Maybe Gerald was used to coming in. Maybe this was his typical way to spend a Sunday.

If so, she felt bad that she hadn't been more welcoming to someone Miss April was so fond of.

Miss April hadn't left her with any special instructions for the neighbor. In fact, if she recalled correctly, she had simply said he had just moved in.

Maybe he was lonely and needed a friend in town. She chastised herself for not being friendlier or more welcoming. And she made up her mind, as she got dressed, that she would do better, not allowing him to disconcert her or put her off her guard. As he had already done.

Thankfully, when she walked out, and maybe a little to her surprise, he was in the exact same position that he had been when she had left.

It didn't look like he had moved a muscle.

She half expected him to have the remote in one hand and the TV on while he flipped through the channels. That's how casual and relaxed he seemed, but maybe he hadn't thought of it, because the TV was off, although he looked at her expectantly as she walked into the room.

"You smell better," he said and then laughed like it was a great joke.

She figured she probably did, and she also reminded herself that she had just decided that she was going to be kind to him and not assume that he meant that as an insult.

She tried to laugh, but it came out more like a couple of sick grunts. "It's such a nice evening, how about we go out on the porch and sit there for a while?"

"I hate sitting out in the evening. The mosquitoes here are terrible. They'll eat me alive."

"Are you sure? I really don't recall having a problem with them when I was sitting out there yesterday." She gave him her most beguiling smile. "Let me get some tea and we'll try it. If it's too much, we can go somewhere else."

She really wanted to get him out of the house. If he stayed here, who knew how long he would be here, and she wasn't sure she was up to entertaining him the entire evening, although—she reminded herself—she would be welcoming and kind.

With a glass of tea in each hand, she gave him a friendly look as she walked through the living room, not giving him a chance to turn her down, but using her hip to push the screen door open, and waiting while he sighed and then pushed up from the couch.

"What is the rate of West Nile virus in this area?" he asked as he walked out the door.

A hypochondriac? She tried not to use that information to her advantage. But she couldn't stop herself from saying, "I think there've been several cases this year. But I could be wrong."

It wasn't lying, and she added that she could be wrong, right?

His lips pressed together, but he didn't excuse himself to go home.

"The swing is so comfortable," she said as she stood beside it, waiting for him to sit down.

She handed him his tea and then went over and sat on the step.

She hoped she hadn't angered him, but there was no way she wanted to get stuck on the swing with him.

His actions were feeling a bit too much of him being in her space for her to choose to sit beside him.

There was just something about him that made her uncomfortable. And while she hadn't used those instincts much in her life, she felt like she could trust them.

"Are you serious?" he asked, setting his tea aside and pulling his phone out of his pocket. "I can Google it. I can't take a chance with my health. These things are serious."

"Yes, please do. I'm curious too." She tried to sound curious, but it was a stretch.

She had never considered West Nile virus and highly doubted that it was an issue in North Dakota.

"I think probably you have a better chance of being attacked by a moose. Or a runaway cow," she added as an afterthought, remembering the fact that Billy and his porcine cohort ran around town unrestrained.

"There was a cow running around earlier. I saw it from my living room window. I thought surely someone was going to get it and put it where it belongs. Do you mean to tell me that this happens all the time?" Gerald seemed truly concerned.

"Yeah. That cow's been running loose for a while now. No one really knows whose it is."

"People just let it run around? Isn't someone going to...I don't know, take it to the Humane Society or something?"

"So it can be adopted?" she asked.

"Or put down." Gerald sounded like that was a normal thing.

"I think the town kind of likes it. That and the pig gives us a little bit of a uniqueness that's fun and makes us stand out from other small towns."

"I don't understand why a town would want to stand out like that. Animals are not meant to be wandering the streets. Before you know it, you have a whole herd of them, and it's dangerous. Actually, speaking of dangerous, it had monstrous horns. It's going to hurt someone. Maybe I should call the police and have them take care of it, if no one else is going to."

"Actually, Sweet Water isn't big enough to have their own police force. There's really not much crime to speak of, so we don't see police around much. You might have a hard time getting them to come out over a cow and a pig that aren't doing anything but minding their own business."

"And wandering around the town where they have no business being. It is disconcerting that people would just look the other way and not do something about that."

Teagan leaned her head back against the porch post and took a sip of her tea. She didn't want to argue about it. She liked the cow and the pig and smiled when she saw them. People were feeding them and had named them as well.

It wouldn't have been hard to get someone to take them home, to give them a home, or to eat them, but it was just nice to have them around.

But she knew she wasn't going to be able to explain that to the man sitting in front of her, so she didn't bother to try.

She wondered how long it would be before she would be able to get up and excuse herself to go inside and close the door before he could follow her in.

Chapter 12

June picked up the empty plate in front of her daughter, Juliann, and her husband, Wayne.

"Would you like some dessert? I made your favorite." She spoke to Wayne but glanced over at Juliann, who shook her head.

"You made my favorite?"

"Yes. The cherry meringue dessert your mother made for your birthday."

"That stuff was goopy. That's not my favorite."

"Oh. I'm sorry. I thought it was." He had said it was at the time. She remembered distinctly asking his mother for the recipe and copying it down in her recipe book, because Wayne had said he liked it.

"I don't care if you ever serve that stuff again. It was disgusting."

June pressed her lips tight to keep from saying anything and carried his plate silently to the kitchen.

She had made it today thinking he would enjoy it.

Lord? I'm trying. Do You see me trying?

Walking back in, she put a smile on her face, reminding herself that she was to love and serve her husband like he was Jesus. The Bible didn't say anything about giving a person an excuse if they were with someone who was unkind to them. In fact, the Bible said being kind to someone who was unkind was like heaping coals of fire on their head.

She didn't really want to hurt her husband, but sometimes she thought that maybe some fiery coals might remind him that other people had feelings too.

"Would you like to take a drive? It's a beautiful day," she said as she lifted the casserole from the table, waiting with it in her hands while he shook his head.

"No. You can go for a drive if you want to, but I don't have time. I have things I need to do."

"Would you like me to help you?"

He laughed. "Unless you've all of a sudden become a master welder, there's nothing you can do."

"Well, I can't weld," she said, smiling and trying to hide the disappointment she felt.

He never wanted to do anything with her.

"May I be excused, please?" Juliann asked.

"Where do you want to go in such a big rush?"

"I have schoolwork to do," Juliann said, her eyes meeting her father's but her body language saying she wanted to get up and leave.

June listened as she walked into the kitchen. Normally Wayne was very dismissive of their children. Occasionally he was unkind, and at that point, even though she figured it probably wasn't biblical, she tried to step in.

"Stupid schoolwork. You're just wasting your time. You need to be out doing something. You're living here rent free. What are you doing to earn your keep?"

Juliann didn't say anything, although she could have made the case that she cooked three nights a week and cleaned on Saturdays, as well as going with June to her cleaning jobs during the summer.

She didn't. She was old enough to know there was no point in trying to reason with her father.

June's oldest daughter had always fought with her dad, and June had hated every second of it. Not that she blamed her daughter, but she hated the contention in her house. They were too much alike, and it was almost a relief when her daughter moved out. The other two had been much less likely to confront their father and just allowed his words to run off them.

Her second daughter had moved out as soon as she could, and she figured Juliann would do the same. No one could stand to live with him for long.

No one except for June.

She had been with him for almost three decades.

Lord, I have been faithful. You say You reward faithfulness. I'm counting on that. Counting on You keeping Your promise. Protect my children.

She always asked God to protect her children and to fill in any gaps where she wasn't enough for them. If there was anything that June wasn't sure of, it was that she didn't know if Wayne's unkindness would adversely affect her children when they got older.

She tried to teach them that sometimes God put hard people in their lives so that they could learn to love despite people being unkind.

There were lots of other lessons a person could learn, like dying to self and giving up their "rights" in order to do something someone else's way. Being gracious and kind in the face of unkindness.

Maybe she'd made a big mistake, but she hoped rather than a big mistake, she taught her children to live according to what the Bible said and not according to what the world said.

That's what she hoped anyway. Only time would tell, but God knew she was doing the best she could. Hopefully, he filled in any gaps for her, but she never expected her children's lives to be perfection, because she knew that they would be dealing with hardship. She also taught them that hardship made a person stronger, as long as they bent with it and didn't get brittle or bitter.

She just hoped the same thing was true for her, because in the back of her head, a little voice always whispered that maybe divorce was the answer. After all, surely it was easier to live without a man constantly criticizing and belittling her than it was to smile and love him anyway.

But she had never been one to take the easy way out.

Wayne finally excused Juliann from the table as June walked back in.

"I'm going to need some welding rods from the hardware store. You can run in and get those for me and drop them off at the shop," Wayne said as he stood up from the table, his boots clomping on the floor as he walked around the edge of the table toward the door.

"Is there a certain size?"

"I'll text what I need to you."

"All right."

While she was doing that, she could take the cherry dessert she made to Teagan. She was housesitting and might appreciate a little gift of food. If nothing else, Deuce was always with Teagan, and he'd help her eat it.

She'd drop it off on her way to get the welding rods.

"Don't turn the air up again, it was way too hot in the house last night when I got home," Wayne said just before he opened the door and walked out.

She had been trying to save money on the electric bill, not to mention he always had it so cold that she could hardly stand it. Even now, she had a sweatshirt and long pants on, as well as a winter vest underneath, trying to stay warm, even though it was the middle of June.

He hadn't waited for an answer, and she didn't give him one, wrapping up the dessert with aluminum foil and grabbing her purse after telling Juliann where she was going and offering to take her with her.

Juliann declined, and June walked out the door herself.

It didn't take long to get to Miss April's house, it was just a short drive, and she parked along the street.

At first, she thought the man on the swing was Deuce, since wherever Teagan was, Deuce was usually close by. But as she got closer, she realized she recognized him as the new fellow in town, and she smiled, glad she would get to meet him sooner rather than later.

"Good afternoon. It's a nice day for sitting on the porch," she said as she walked up to Miss April's house carrying her dessert.

"It sure is. A beautiful evening."

"The mosquitoes are terrible. I must have gotten bit six times since we sat down," the man said, slapping at his arm and spilling the tea he held in his hand.

"That's too bad. I brought you some dessert." She held it out to Teagan, who stood with a smile.

"Thank you so much!" She sniffed, even though the container was covered with aluminum foil. "Is this the cherry dessert that you brought the last time we had a luncheon at the church?"

"It sure is."

"That's fantastic! It was so good! I loved it."

"Good to hear."

"I'll have to try that. I never was very fond of cherry, but I can give that a shot," Gerald said, and June wasn't sure what it was, whether it was a micro expression that blinked across Teagan's face, or whether it was the stiffening of her shoulders. Something elusive, but very real, made June think that Gerald had overstayed his welcome.

When Teagan stood holding the dessert and didn't invite anyone in, June was almost sure of it.

Finally, Teagan said, "I think I saw some paper plates inside. I can go and get them and grab some spoons, if you all want to have some on the porch with me?"

"I'd rather go in. These mosquitoes are terrible."

"I'd like to stay out." Teagan didn't say anything more, and she didn't confront Gerald exactly, but she definitely didn't sound eager to spend any more time with him.

"I'm sorry. I need to do a parts run for my husband. I can't stay. But I hope you enjoy."

Teagan nodded, and June could see past the strained smile. She felt a little guilty at leaving Teagan alone, but she didn't waste any time when she got in her car.

Pulling out her phone, she dialed Deuce's number, which she happened to have since he was the one who plowed their driveway last winter, and she often called him, at her husband's bequest, to find out when he would be there.

She had her phone on hands' free as she pulled out on the road.

"Hello?" Deuce answered.

"Deuce. I was surprised to see Teagan in town without you."

"I'm watching Minnie today. Teagan went for a ride with us, and we had a picnic together, but she's watching Miss April's house in town, and we didn't want to take Minnie there without talking to Miss April first."

"I'm sure Miss April wouldn't mind," June said easily, confident that what she was saying was true.

"We didn't think so either, but we figured it would be rude not to ask first."

"Well, whether you can find someone to help you with Minnie or not, I think Teagan could use some rescuing."

"Rescuing?" There was a new tone in Deuce's voice. A tone of concern and maybe a little alarm. That did not surprise June at all.

"The neighbor's there. I'm guessing he's overstaying his welcome. He seems...very interested in Teagan."

"Thanks. I'll be right in."

Deuce didn't even say goodbye as the line went dead.

June smiled. She had thought she had known her husband before they got married, but part of that was him putting on a front and part of that was her imagining they had a far better relationship than what they actually did. She could take all the blame for it and just say she made a foolish choice. But all that aside, anyone could see that Teagan and Deuce were made for each other, and she was sure she had done the right thing by calling Deuce just now.

Regardless, the whole thing had given her a smile, and as she pulled into the hardware store, she could almost forget that her life was a long way from what she had hoped it would be when she had married with stars in her eyes almost three decades ago.

But that didn't mean that she couldn't be happy for other people and couldn't do a little matchmaking when the situation called for it. After all, Charlene might have hung up her matchmaking hat, but Miss April, and Helen and June, were the unofficial inheritors of it.

Maybe she was wrong, but she was pretty sure that she had done the exact right thing, and she couldn't deny that it made her feel amazing. Maybe doing something to help two people who were perfect for each other get together helped her feel better about the mess of her own relationship.

Chapter 13

Deuce checked his speed again, trying to keep it under the speed limit. He wasn't worried about Teagan, exactly. But maybe it was a little bit of the feeling that he'd been having... Was it jealousy? He didn't like the idea of Gerald pushing his way in with her. Maybe she was enjoying his company? The thought sent cold chills down his back, as much as he didn't want to admit that it did.

And made his foot push harder on the gas pedal as well. He again had to deliberately make himself pull up.

Teagan could choose whomever she wanted to. And he truly, truly wanted her to be happy. If she was happy with someone else, he wouldn't stand in her way.

But he would also get there as fast as he could, just in case she didn't want someone else, and he was being a pain.

He parked right in front of Miss April's house and had barely turned the truck off before he hopped out and strode around.

The porch was empty, and he took the steps two at a time, knocking on the door before opening it without waiting for an answer.

He could tell as soon as he saw Teagan that there had been a problem.

Her face was scrunched up, and her body was pulled away as Gerald stood in front of her. He wasn't touching her, and his hands were at his sides, but he was closer than Teagan preferred.

She was friendly and outgoing, kind and sweet, but she had a thing about her personal space.

Especially with strangers.

Typically he got a pass for that, as did anyone who was close to her. But she always put more than enough padding between her and someone else. She said it was a weird touch thing she had, and he never questioned it. Typically it wasn't an issue.

Regardless, the pinched look on her face gave way to relief as she recognized him when he walked in the door.

"Teagan. Sorry I'm late. I know we had plans this evening," he said slowly, knowing she would go along with whatever he said and hoping his initial assessment—that Teagan was upset and Gerald was unwelcome—was accurate.

"Yes! I thought maybe you had forgotten."

"You have plans? You didn't say."

"You didn't ask," she said, scrunching her shoulder into herself as she walked around Gerald and practically flew into Deuce's arms.

He caught her, realizing she trembled. He didn't typically hold her. Their friendship never really called for hugs, but he pulled her tight, wondering if the trembling was because of Gerald or something else. Something he didn't know about. Maybe something unrelated to the situation he'd walked in on.

"Well, now you know, so it's nice to see you, and I guess we'll see you around sometime. I think you can make it home by yourself. It's not a long walk."

Deuce grabbed the door, keeping one arm around Teagan, keeping her close to him, as he indicated the open doorway with a nod of his head.

At first, he thought Gerald was going to dig in, and Deuce didn't want to have to let go of Teagan in order to deal with it, but he would have.

But after a moment's hesitation, Gerald inclined his head and started walking toward the door.

When he got even with Deuce and Teagan, he said, "I'll be back over tomorrow. We can continue our conversation then. I was having a good time."

"We're busy tomorrow too." Deuce spoke before Teagan could. If she wanted to, later she could tell Gerald that they shifted plans and she could spend the day with him anyway. But for now, he wanted to make it clear that the choice was Teagan's, and she got to say whether or not they were going to spend the day together. Gerald wouldn't be inviting himself into her life without any say from her.

Against him, Teagan relaxed just a bit, and Deuce felt like he had made the right decision.

He barely waited for Gerald to walk out the door before he closed it behind him.

"Thank you," Teagan said as he put his other arm around her and held her close.

He didn't say anything else, just held her, waiting for her to relax enough to tell him what was going on.

He was pretty sure she was okay and holding her own, but he wanted to hear it from her. Just to know for sure that he was right.

Finally, she pulled back a little but kept her arms on either side of him. "How did you know?"

"Miss June called me. She said she didn't think Gerald was a welcome visitor. That's all I needed to hear."

"What about Minnie?"

"Brooklyn was home, and I pretty much dropped Minnie on her and ran."

"I'll have to thank Brooklyn."

"I don't think you need to. She hadn't made it into town to talk to Miss Charlene yet, and she told me that she thought maybe it would go better if she took Minnie. She thought she might look more pitiful with a child in tow than she would just going by herself."

"I guess Charlene is pretty imposing, even to those of us who don't seem like we would be affected by it."

"Oh, I think Brooklyn is affected all right. It wouldn't shock me at all if she ends up in the kissing booth, despite all her bluster about telling Charlene she's not going to do it."

Teagan giggled. "I think you're right. And I wouldn't be the slightest bit surprised if she ends up in it with Cormac. She might as well just suck it up and accept the fact that the town wants the two of them to be together."

"If they kiss and make up, people will leave them alone."

As Deuce was saying that, he wondered if the same was true for Teagan and him. If they finally became a couple or at least allowed the town to think they were, maybe people in town would stop asking them when they were going to get together.

It was an idea worth considering, and he wanted to run it by Teagan, but not yet.

"I want to hear what was happening here."

"All right. I'll tell you. If you take me for ice cream."

"Really? You drive a hard bargain, lady."

"I need ice cream after the events of this evening."

"That bad?"

"No. Just stressful. And I haven't seen Cordilia since this morning. I didn't want to look for her too much in front of Gerald. I wasn't sure if Gerald would go to Miss April and tell her that I'd lost the cat. Which, I really haven't. I just haven't seen her."

"You mean him."

"Right. It's so odd that she would name her male cats female names."

They spent some time looking around the house, under the furniture, behind it, and anywhere else they could think of to look, but Cordilia was nowhere in sight. He didn't come to his name, either, although Deuce thought that was typical for cats. Normally they didn't come despite people calling their names.

He could be wrong, because he certainly wasn't an expert on cats.

Despite twenty minutes of searching, they couldn't find the cat anywhere.

"Do you think it might have run out when I wasn't looking?"

"Was there any time you had the door open and weren't looking?" he asked, having a hard time imagining that the cat could slip out without her noticing. Especially considering how conscientious Teagan usually was. She wouldn't have opened the door without paying attention.

"No. But I did take a shower while Gerald was here."

"He was here while you showered?" Deuce couldn't believe that. He supposed that incredulity came out in his tone.

"He invited himself in when I got home from your house. We had ridden horses, and I smelled like it. I didn't want to tell him to leave, couldn't figure out how without being rude, and he didn't offer to when I said I needed to shower. So... I did, and he sat here in the living room. As far as I know, he was on the couch the whole time."

"He was in the same spot when you came back?"

"Exactly the same spot. I... I thought about not going, because I don't know him well enough to know whether I can trust him to be alone. But I did."

"I hardly think he would get off the couch and open the door just to let the cat out, and you've barely seen the cat. I can't believe it would come out while he was here and you weren't."

"I agree with that. That's kind of what I was thinking. I mean, after all, he doesn't seem to be an animal person."

"No. He didn't strike me that way either. He struck me as a very self-absorbed, concerned-for-himself kind of person." Deuce wouldn't say that to just anyone, but he knew Teagan would understand that he wasn't being unkind to Gerald, just giving his honest opinion.

"Yeah. That's what I got out of it too."

"How about we go get ice cream, you can tell me what all happened, and we'll come back and maybe the cat will come out from wherever he's hiding."

"Well, I'd like to be optimistic, but I'm feeling like he's not in the house. But I think ice cream will make me feel better. At least it will give me energy to keep looking."

They shared a smile before they walked to the door.

Chapter 14

Deuce opened the door, and Teagan walked out ahead of him.

"There you two are. You're finally together. Is it a Sunday night date?"

They hadn't even gotten off the porch, and Mrs. Cella strolled by, pulling a wagon with her granddaughter in it.

"No. We're still just friends. Going for ice cream."

Deuce didn't say anything, but he nodded beside Teagan, because he would never not support her.

They stepped off the porch and went in the opposite direction as Mrs. Cella.

They'd taken three steps before Deuce decided he might as well broach the subject. He wanted to do it carefully, because everything he'd said to Aspen, everything about not wanting to mess up the great relationship that he had with Teagan, was still true.

But he thought that maybe he and Teagan could talk about this. If he was careful.

But first, he wanted to know what happened. "Tell me what was going on between you and Gerald."

"There is nothing going on with me. Gerald seemed a little...stalkerish. He invited himself in, then he wouldn't leave. Not that I asked him to, just...he sat there and sat there and, I don't know, I just never asked him to stay. It was weird."

"Yeah. You think he'd take a hint, but apparently he can't."

"Right. So, I delayed going in as much as I could, even after Miss June left. I kept thinking that he'd leave. Or, at the very least, not follow me in. But he ended up in the house when I went to get silverware for the dessert that Miss June brought. I set it down on the counter and turned around to ask him if he wanted a big piece or a small piece, and that's when he walked over and stopped right in front of me." Teagan shivered, and for the first time since Deuce could remember, he was tempted to take her hand. Even more tempted to put his arm around her.

But he didn't.

"So you know if that happens again, you can text me. I'll come as soon as I get your message," he said.

"I know. I just knew you had Minnie, and I hated to bother you. I didn't realize he was going to crowd me like that. He was annoying on the porch but not...in my space."

"I saw he was in your space. I know how that bothers you."

"Yeah." She looked over at him, and they shared an understanding glance. The kind of look a person has with someone they know backwards and forwards and inside out.

It was a comforting kind of look, the kind he liked sharing. Because they made him feel like he was with someone who knew him, truly knew him, and loved him anyway. That's how he felt about Teagan.

He felt like this might be a good time to broach the other subject. He took a breath and then plunged in.

"So... Do you remember what we said about Brooklyn and Cormac?" he asked, waiting for Teagan to shift gears in her head. Usually she followed him pretty well, but this felt a little outside his comfort zone, and he wasn't sure whether it would be so unusual that she wouldn't understand.

But she got him, like she always did.

"Yeah. That if they just bit the bullet and kiss and make up, the townspeople would stop bothering them and trying to put them together?"

"Yeah, that."

"You think that would work?"

"I don't know. I think it would be worth a try. But I wasn't really thinking about Brooklyn and Cormac."

"You weren't?"

"I was thinking about us."

There. The words were out.

"Us?"

She was going to make him explain it.

"Yeah. Just like Brooklyn and Cormac, people give them a hard time and are pushing them together because they resist it. I wondered if people give us a hard time about being a couple because we resist it."

She walked in silence for a bit, as though digesting this, and then she said, very carefully, "I suppose that could be true."

"So, I was thinking, what would you think about…us surprising the town, or maybe not surprising them, by actually becoming a couple?"

As he said the words, and he thought about his argument, he realized that he maybe made one serious error.

He was thinking like a man.

The whole thing had been thought out the way a man would think. He hadn't considered how it would sound to Teagan.

"You…want to pretend to be a couple so that the townspeople will stop bugging us about it?"

Yeah. She didn't sound excited about it at all. She didn't even sound like she thought it was a good idea. In fact, she wasn't even trying to sound encouraging. Which is what she usually did, even when he had terrible ideas. She might tell him it was a terrible idea, but if he was bound and determined to do it, she would throw in behind him and help him however she could.

He wasn't getting that vibe with this.

What he should have done, now that he thought about it, was go at it from a romantic perspective, at least let her know that he admired her and was interested in more. That was true. He admired her, even loved her, maybe not in a romantic sense exactly, but he felt like he could go there. But that was what he was afraid of. Those were the words that he was afraid would ruin their friendship.

He pulled himself back, reminding himself that their friendship was the most important thing. He had rationalized everything, and he needed to follow his plan. Not panic and think like a woman.

"It's like this. Everywhere we go, pretty much everyone always asks us when we're going to be a couple. If we just...act like we're a couple, people will stop asking us about it."

"I see. I... I suppose that would work."

"If you're not sure about it, there's no pressure. I just was thinking about it. Seems like everybody I meet anytime I go anywhere, they're always asking if you and I are together yet. It just got me thinking."

"I guess that's true. People ask me that all the time too. And this might be a good time to experiment with it because it would keep Gerald from bothering me."

"Exactly. That's a great point. I hadn't even thought of that, but it's a good idea."

They stopped at the ice-cream stand, and both of them got a small cone, Teagan chocolate and Deuce vanilla.

They turned and walked slowly back toward Miss April's house.

"I guess the most important thing to me whether we decide to do that or not is I don't want it to affect our friendship. That's what I've always said to people when they've asked me about it. That our friendship was more important than any kind of romantic relationship."

"That's what I always tell people too. But since we both know that we're just doing this to kind of keep people off our backs, there shouldn't be any problem with it."

"So... Nothing will change?"

"Well, I probably should hold your hand, maybe put my arm around you. Maybe we should do some kissing, but nothing too radical."

"Okay." She sounded uncertain.

"What? Are you scared?" He grinned over at her, his carefree, devil-may-care grin, but hers was wobbly in return.

He shifted his ice-cream cone to his other hand and used his free hand to grab hers. "There. Like that. Is that so terrible?"

She took a few more steps, looking thoughtful, almost playfully thoughtful. She grinned. "I actually like it."

"Me too." That was true. He did. Funny that Teagan's hand felt so perfect in his. He walked a few more steps before he said, "Maybe we should try the kissing thing. Just try it and see. If we don't like it, no one has to know."

"All right. I suppose that sounds like a good idea. We should see if we can stand to kiss each other before we actually have to do it in front of anyone. That way we'll know. And we can stop this farce in its tracks if it's not something that's going to work out."

"Exactly." He squeezed her hand, and she squeezed his back, and they went the rest of the way to Miss April's house, their ice-cream cones both gone by the time they got back.

"Do you suppose we should practice now?" he asked as they reached the porch.

"Let's start with a hug," she said, looking up at him. Some of the old fire was back in her eyes, but she looked worried too.

"Like we hugged earlier?" he prompted her, thinking maybe she had forgotten that she had run to him and grabbed a hold of him and they had shared a hug already that evening.

"Oh. I forgot about that. Thank you. Thank you for not making it weird. In fact, you made it so normal that it didn't even register."

"I'm glad I made a lasting impression on you."

"No. That's what I'm saying. It just felt right. Kind of the way holding hands with you does."

They were facing each other, and instead of answering him, she stepped closer, putting her hands on either side of his waist.

He held still, trying not to move, as though moving would make her change her mind. He definitely didn't want that.

"This feels weird," she finally said.

"As in compared to other men's waists? Or as in because it's me?" He tried not to hold his breath, but he found himself barely breathing as he waited for her reply. He wanted her to feel comfortable. Comfortable enough that she would stop holding onto his waist and slide her hands the whole way around him.

"Not weird in a bad way. Weird in a I'm not used to this kind of way, but I kind of like it." There was a little smile on her lips, and after a few moments, she finally did what he had been longing for her to do, and that was step closer, putting her hands the whole way around him.

"Is this okay?" He put his hands on her shoulders.

"Yes." She replied without hesitation.

"And this?" He slid his arms around her back and pulled her close.

"I can't even say how perfect that feels."

But rather than lifting her head and reaching up, she turned it to the side and laid it on his chest. "Maybe we can just get used to this for now and do the kissing thing later?"

"That's a good idea. After all, we don't want to rush anything." And, in his opinion, a kiss could completely change their relationship. While holding hands, even hugging, was almost benign. People did it every day. Just because those people weren't Teagan and him didn't mean anything. Or maybe it did.

Regardless, Teagan was far more important to him than what the townspeople thought, or trying to prove anything by kissing her, or not even trying to prove anything but doing it because he wanted to.

Which he found he did. Very much.

But if she didn't want to, or if she just wasn't ready, he wanted to wait. Because he knew instinctively he would not enjoy anything that she wasn't completely on board with.

"I think your idea of waiting was a good one," he murmured. No matter how badly he didn't want to wait.

"I'm a little scared. Not of you," she hastened to add, because she must have felt him stiffen. He didn't want to scare her. And it shocked him a little that she would say that.

He relaxed. "What are you scared of?"

"It's just a change. You know? Sometimes changes are scary, even when they are changes that we're excited about or that we want or look forward to."

"I know. We've been through a lot of changes together."

"We sure have. I can't imagine my life without you. When I think back to all the things I've done, all the big times in my life, you've always been there. There is no single thing that happened to me that you weren't with me in it and through it. It's…uncanny how we've been together so much, and I never even really thought about it."

"Me, either. Not until the last few days. And I realize that my friendship with you is one of the most important things in my life. And I didn't think you knew it."

"I think I probably did. But you know how you know something, but someone saying it just confirms it?"

"Yeah. I know."

"That's what I needed from you. Just to hear it."

"Meow."

That one sound broke whatever spell had settled around them, and both of their heads jerked toward the screen door which was still shut. They'd left the heavy door open, since they were just walking two blocks down the street, and Sweet Water wasn't exactly a place where they needed to worry about someone breaking in.

"It's Cordilia!" Teagan said, moving away from him, quickly, but then slowing as she carefully opened the door.

"Be careful he doesn't run out," he cautioned, needlessly, because she was being very, very careful.

"Oh, my goodness. I thought for sure I had lost him. I thought I was going to have to explain to Miss April how I had done my best, but I just hadn't seen him, and I didn't know when he got out and I wasn't sure how to find him, and I could just see me combing the streets of Sweet Water and not being able to find him anywhere."

He laughed, because it was such a run-on sentence, and she was obviously so relieved.

He sank to his knees beside Teagan as they petted the cat together, who had somehow forgotten that he was supposed to be shy and was enjoying all the attention.

"Thank you," she said, looking over at him. "Thank you for supporting me, no matter whether I am resisting changes or looking for a lost cat."

"Whether I'm watching a two-year-old or breaking a wild horse."

They shared a smile, and Deuce kind of thought something shifted in their relationship, something good. He looked forward to what their future brought.

Chapter 15

Deuce parked his truck at his family's house, a smile still lifting the corners of his mouth.

He'd had the best time with Teagan, and excitement about their future, despite the unknowns, made his heart beat a little faster than normal.

Could he have everything?

Maybe the more pressing question was, did they want everything? Did they want to take their relationship from friendship to something even more?

They hadn't really answered those questions. Maybe they never would. Maybe just staying right where they were was the best idea and they would both wake up in the morning and realize that.

But for right now, his mind and heart were alive with possibilities. So much so that he didn't notice his parents' car was parked in front of the house until he was at the walk.

Normally they spent the entire week in Fargo, only coming home on weekends occasionally.

His sisters, Kennedy and Malley, stayed in Fargo with them while Aspen and Deuce stayed on the farm, taking care of the animals and also dealing with any problems that arose at their warehouse outside of Sweet Water.

It was very odd for his parents to be home on a Sunday night.

A bit of dread pushed down the excitement that had been spiraling in his stomach. He wanted to shove it away, but he knew it was completely grounded in reality. If his parents were home, there was probably a problem somewhere.

He opened the door, and the smell of home, mixed with spaghetti sauce and spices, drew him in.

"Smells like someone's cooking in here," he commented as he walked in the door and closed it behind him.

"Deuce! I was getting ready to text you. I figured you and Teagan were doing something, but we need to talk to you." His mother, an apron tied around her waist, came around the corner of the kitchen and greeted him with a smile.

"Hey, Mom," he said. "Good to see you." He spoke like nothing was wrong. "Give me a minute to get my boots off, and I'll be in."

"All right. Dad's in here, along with your sisters. We were just waiting on you."

Oh great. A family meeting. At least there was going to be food, and good food from the smell of it.

He had just toed his other boot off when Minnie came running around the corner.

"DD!" she said as she ran into his arms.

He caught her, hopping on one foot until he regained his balance and finished shaking his boot off. "You again. What are you doing here?"

She laughed. "I live here! What are you doing here?"

"I live here too. Funny we keep meeting each other like this."

She laughed and nodded her head, like she understood what he was saying.

He shifted her to one hip and carried her into the kitchen with him. "So something must be up, since you guys are here on a Sunday night," he started as he walked into the kitchen. He wasn't going to pretend he thought everything was okay. Still, he walked over and gave Kennedy and Malley both a side-arm hug, keeping Minnie on one hip while he did it.

"We can't have a family meal together?" his mom asked with her brows raised, a wooden spoon in one hand.

"Is that what this is?" he asked.

"No. You're right to think that there is more going on here," his dad said, coming over and shaking his hand. His dad held a knife in one hand, and half an onion was chopped on the cutting board on the counter.

"Looks like everybody's helping to cook. Is there a job for me?" Deuce asked.

"If you're holding Minnie, that's a job enough," Kennedy said, making a face at Minnie, which Minnie returned.

He wanted to ask about Minnie's parents, but he didn't want to do that in front of her. She was young and most likely wouldn't understand the adult conversation around her, but he didn't know exactly what she would pick up on, and he didn't want to upset her in case something was seriously wrong.

He didn't think that was what the family meeting was about, but maybe it was.

"Let me have her," Aspen said, coming over and holding her hands out for Minnie. "We'll go outside and play for a little bit. We can see the chicks." She smiled engagingly at Minnie, who reluctantly let go of Deuce and slid into Aspen's arms.

Deuce watched her walk out, assuming that whatever they were going to talk about either she already knew, or she at least knew that it wasn't going to be affecting her.

"All right, spit it out. I know something's up." He leaned back against the counter and crossed his arms over his chest. In the back of his head, the thought crossed his mind that he wished Teagan were here. His parents would talk in front of her, she was almost like part of the family. But it was a little late to invite her. Plus, at his age he needed to be able to handle his family and their news without her.

"There's no bad news," his mother said right away with a reassuring smile.

"Nothing bad, just changes. We want you to be involved in them," his dad added, pausing as he sliced the onion.

"I think changes are good." He liked the changes that were happening with him and Teagan, and it seemed interesting that there would be changes in his family at the same time.

"You know there have been some shake-ups in the supervisor positions at our warehouse here in Sweet Water. We're pulling our experienced supervisor from Fargo and putting him in charge of Sweet Water. Even though Fargo is a bigger town, our Sweet Water facility does four times as much business."

His dad wasn't telling him anything he didn't already know. Deuce nodded and waited.

"What we want is for you to move to Fargo and take over the open position in that warehouse. With your dad and I there, even though you don't have any experience, we can guide you along. It'll be easy for you to pick up, and you'll be running it like a pro in no time." His mom glanced up at him, lifting her brows and giving him an easy smile, like she hadn't just shifted his world.

His parents wanted him to move?

Growing up in his family, he'd always helped in the business. It was just part of life. The same way with helping on the farm. They all pulled together. A lot of families weren't like that, where parents went to a nine-to-five job, came home, and didn't have anything invested in their work. But with his family, their work was their family's livelihood, and everyone knew it and helped.

He'd never turned them down when they'd asked him to do anything. Thankfully, they usually took into account their kids' aptitudes and interests, and in the case of Aspen, who was a homebody, and him, who enjoyed working with the horses and on the ranch, they'd ended up staying home and taking care of things here. Which was perfect for their personalities. While Kennedy and Malley, who were both more go-getters, had been involved in the business in a more people-oriented way. Kennedy oversaw the office and paperwork, and Malley was their HR department.

Because Deuce was able to do a lot of the IT work from home, he had added that to his schedule over the years, but he had never been the slightest bit interested in moving or in any kind of on-site, in-person position, like a supervisor's position would require.

He tried not to look as dismayed as he felt. He couldn't tell his parents an outright no, but he wanted to.

"What your father left out is that our warehouse in Fargo is struggling. We really need to pitch in in order to save it." His mom's words hit like rocks, then the kitchen was quiet.

His parents had worked hard, he'd seen it over the years. They'd taught all of their kids to have a great work ethic as well, and while they'd worked hard, they'd all taken time to play too.

Because his parents had been so flexible in what they'd allowed him to do, he'd ended up with the very best life possible. Being able to train horses, which wasn't always a lucrative business, and certainly he couldn't afford to pay for a ranch just with the money he made on that alone. But what his parents allowed him to do had been to work the job of his heart, work another job that wasn't too bad, and make enough to enjoy his life.

Now they were asking for him to make a small sacrifice. When he'd never had to sacrifice anything before, other than time.

How could he turn them down after all they'd done for him?

"We didn't come here this evening expecting you to make a decision right away. We know this is a big move. We also know that it's not necessarily what you want to do. Hopefully it will be a temporary thing. Although, by temporary, I'm thinking at least a year and a half or two years, in order to pull this warehouse up and make it profitable."

"What makes you think that I even have the skills to do that? I've never been in a supervising position. I don't know anything about it."

"Of course you don't. But you're honest and trustworthy. That's part of the problem. We've had two supervisors now who have not had the company's best interest at heart, only their own. And who have done favors for their cronies and not done their job. We know you're more than capable of taking over, and we also know that we can trust that if you say you've done something, it's been done. We do have safeguards in place, but a smart con artist can work his way around those. As we've seen." His dad's lips flattened as he chopped the last of the onion, setting the knife down and looking Deuce straight in the eye. "We need you, son. Just for two years. Give us that much, then you can come back to the ranch. We've actually been working on a deal where we'll give you housing and a daily allowance, and at the end of the two years, we'll put your name on the deed to the ranch."

That was intriguing. Very tempting as well.

He only had to move away for two years, and then the ranch would be in his name too.

"But again, you don't have to make a decision today. We figure two weeks would be enough time to think about it, and if you need a little longer once you've decided to take the job to take care of your horses or find someone else to do that, that would be fine. We're looking at a month, no more, till we need you in Fargo." His mom's words were soft, not demanding, but matter-of-fact as well.

He heard that they needed him. He figured that's probably exactly what she wanted him to hear.

"I assume Aspen would be staying here?" he asked, not really because he was curious, because he figured he already knew the answer, but because he didn't really know what else to say. Other than he'd take the two weeks to think about it. More likely, he'd take the two weeks to talk to Teagan about it.

He could hardly start a new relationship with her when they would be separated for the first time in their lives. The drive to Fargo was hours long, and he wouldn't be coming home every day. It might be a stretch for him to be home every weekend if things were as bad as his parents said. They hadn't mentioned it, but they probably were tapping him because they knew he would be able to work seven days a week, twelve or sixteen or more hours a day, if that was what was necessary.

They couldn't hire someone and expect that kind of commitment and devotion out of them. But out of family? Of course they could. And he would give it. Happily. Because he owed his very life to his parents' businesses.

"She will stay here, as she always has. Kennedy and Malley will both be in Fargo, that's part of the reason that Malley went out last fall. Because things were going bad. But we need everyone to turn the ship around. Everyone except for Aspen, who should be able to handle Sweet Water on her own."

His dad walked over and put a hand on his mom's shoulder. "I'm sure you have a ton of questions, and we're happy to answer whatever you want to ask. And if you need to think about it for a bit, that's fine as well. We don't want to push you into this, if you truly don't want to leave the farm. We know that's always been your wish. But you know we wouldn't ask you to go if it wasn't absolutely necessary."

"I know. That's what I've been thinking. But yeah, this is a big surprise to me. So if you don't mind, I'll think about it for a bit, and I'm sure I'll have questions, but my gut is saying that I'm going to do whatever you need me to do."

He hadn't realized how much tension was in the room until with those words, everyone seemed to breathe a sigh of relief. He probably should look at the financial statements and see exactly where they were, because if there was that much riding on it, and he hadn't even known, he should be more aware of what was going on in the business.

"All right then, let's enjoy our meal together. We don't have to spend the entire evening talking about business and problems," his mom said, her movements much more free and relaxed.

He wasn't looking forward to going to Fargo, and he wanted to talk to Teagan, but he knew she would understand that he really owed his parents and could hardly turn them down.

At least, he hoped she would.

Chapter 16

"Here, take this and get you and Edger an ice cream. Don't lose the change." Travis handed his brother Roger a five-dollar bill.

Conscious that he only had two twenties left in his pocket, and he needed to somehow get groceries for the week, he thought the five dollars was probably worth it, because he wanted to be able to meet Shanna without his brothers bothering him.

She said she would be in town for cheerleading practice at the community center, and that she would take five minutes to meet him behind the shed that sat on the side of the property, near the back of the bakery.

"You don't want any?" Roger asked as they started away.

"No. Just don't lose the change." Travis hadn't had ice cream in a really long time, and he wouldn't have minded having some, but he didn't want his brothers hurrying back to give it to him before it melted.

"Hey," he said, waiting until they turned around. "You take it to the park and eat it. If you get done before I get there, it's okay for you to play, but don't play on the little kid stuff if there's little kids there. And don't break anything."

Edgar gave him a mock salute, while Roger just grinned, before they turned around, taking two walking steps before breaking into a run, an unspoken race to see who could get to the ice-cream store first.

Travis shook his head. His brothers were great, and he loved them, but sometimes they were annoying.

They were especially difficult when he was trying to impress girls.

He only had one more year until he was officially an adult and could get a full-time adult job. He had dreams of moving out, but he probably wouldn't do that. Not as long as his mom continued down the road she was on. Currently she was passed out on their couch, hungover from the night before.

At least somehow her waitressing job in Rockerton managed to pay her gas money, and the rent, as well as finance her drinking issues.

Thankfully, Tadgh had put in a word with Ford Hansen, and Travis worked part-time on Ford's farm, making enough to buy groceries and most of the clothes they needed.

Getting a chance to meet a girl was a pretty big treat. He didn't want his brothers to ruin it. What girl wanted to be with a guy who had two little boys hanging around him? If she knew he was responsible for them, she'd definitely not be interested.

Not to mention, his brothers could be embarrassing. They hadn't quite gotten to the stage where they no longer thought passing gas was funny.

Of course, he hadn't gotten to that stage either, but at least he knew that it didn't impress girls. His brothers hadn't figured that out yet.

Walking down the sidewalk, he cut between the barbershop and the bakery, using the trail that was worn into the ground.

It was in shadow, and at first, he didn't see the figure sitting on the ground.

He took two more steps before he realized it was a person, a girl, and she was crying.

His shoes hadn't made any noise on the hardpacked dirt, and she wasn't looking up but was sitting on the ground, her back against the brick wall of the barbershop, her head on her knees with her arms wrapped around her legs, sobbing.

His first instinct was to turn around and retrace his steps. He didn't want to be involved in whatever problem this girl had.

But he recognized her.

Ellen. Tadgh's daughter. She had been kind to him, along with her uncle Tadgh, and had fed him more than once. She had never complained when her uncle had invited him in for a meal, and as much as a little twelve-year-old could, she'd been a gracious hostess for his brothers and him almost every weekend for the past three summers.

He knew more than once he and his brothers had left and it had been Ellen's job to clean up after them. As far as he knew, she hadn't complained.

Still, she was a little girl, and he didn't feel the same way about her that he felt about Shanna, who was two years older than he was and had already graduated.

She was back from college and had been gathering a volunteer troop of cheerleaders together to practice over the summer.

Something about a state competition or something. He didn't care. He just was happy that she responded to his text and agreed to meet him.

He glanced at his phone quickly. He had five minutes.

He took two steps forward and went down on one knee. "Ellen?"

Her head jerked up, her face red and streaked with tears. Her eyes wide and startled like she hadn't been expecting anyone to see her.

"Are you with Uncle Tadgh?" she asked, her voice hoarse from crying.

"No. I didn't know you two were in town." And then he remembered. "You had to sell Daisy today."

She hiccupped. Her chin trembled, and her eyes filled with tears again as she nodded.

Something warm and strong tugged at his heartstrings to see Ellen, who was usually so happy and sweet, crying and broken-hearted.

He touched her arm. "I know how much you loved her."

She nodded. "I bottle-fed her from the day she was born."

He knew Daisy was an orphan whose mom had died, and he also knew that Ellen had fed her morning and night all through the cold and brutal North Dakota winter.

"I'm sure your uncle sold her to a good home," he said.

She swiped at her tears with the back of her hand, leaving a grimy streak across her cheek. She'd obviously been working, helping Tadgh get Daisy ready to go to her new home. "I know. Uncle Tadgh told me that if I didn't want her to go, I could say so, but I know this is how we make some of our money, and I didn't want to be selfish. I'll have new calves, and the kids who are getting Daisy only have her. It's just... I love her."

He patted her arm awkwardly, not sure of what to say.

"I know." Ellen waved a hand. "I'm dumb for loving a cow."

"No. I don't think so. I think it's wonderful that you love animals, and you're so good with them."

"Do you think so?"

He nodded, although he really hadn't thought too much about it before. He knew she was responsible and that she took care of her animals before she took care of herself. The contrast between this twelve-year-old girl and his own mother couldn't be more stark. His mom was certainly more interested in taking care of herself than she was in taking care of the humans that lived in her house, let alone a cow.

He understood some of the sacrifice involved, since he had been charged with taking care of his brothers for years now. Maybe not charged. He stepped up to the plate, because no one else was doing it.

Every once in a while, he wished someone would take care of him.

That reminded him of Shanna, and he knew he only had a few seconds left before he was going to be late.

"Sometimes we just need a good cry," he said, repeating what his mother had told him when he'd come down to the table at times in the middle of the night and saw her sitting there with her head in her hands, tears dripping onto the wood in front of her.

He hadn't understood then, and he really didn't know that he understood now. Just sometimes a person was sad, and part of that sadness involved crying.

"I'll be fine. You go," Ellen said, almost as though she knew he had some place to be.

"You don't want me?" he asked, trying to tease her a little and maybe get a smile before he left.

"I know you're in town for a reason, and you're cutting through here for a reason as well. You told me once this winter that there was a cheerleader you liked, and I'm betting you're meeting her. Go on. I'll be fine."

He had been getting ready to push up to his feet, but he paused, with both hands on his knees, his elbows out, as he stared at the girl in front of him.

"You actually remember what I told you?" He couldn't remember anyone listening to him like that before.

His mom couldn't remember from one day to the next what he told her, even if it was something as important as them being out of milk and her needing to stop and get some on her way home from work.

But that Ellen had remembered that he had his eye on a cheerleader and had deduced that he might be meeting her was impressive. And he wasn't quite sure what to do with that information. It was new in his world, to have someone who didn't just pay attention to him but wanted him to take care of himself, the way Ellen had just told him to.

Even though she was sitting there crying and obviously needed a friend, she was sending him off to do what she knew he wanted to.

He felt torn, wanting to be the kind of friend Ellen deserved but also wanting to do what she suggested, knowing his opportunity to do so was limited.

Shanna wouldn't be around forever. And Ellen would still be here when he was done.

"You're right. I am meeting someone, but I'll be right back."

She shook her head. "I'll be gone by then. You go. I'm going to be fine. Don't worry about me."

She was right. Shanna was the one he needed to be concerned about right now.

He stood, still feeling in his chest that he was making the wrong decision, but knowing in his mind that it was the right one. If he had any hope of having a relationship with Shanna, she had to be more important to him than a twelve-year-old girl who was way too young for him, who was more like a little sister.

Maybe, if there was enough money left from his groceries, he would see that Ellen got an ice cream before he went home.

"I'll be back," he said, with a last look at the little girl leaning against the wall.

He walked out from between the buildings into the bright sunlight, and it took his eyes a moment to adjust. When they did, he didn't see Shanna at first, his eyes skimming across the parking lot and shed and back before he saw her, long brown hair in a ponytail that hung down her back, leaning against the side of the shed in the shade, her arms crossed over her chest, and one of her long bare legs sticking out with a bent knee as she had one foot propped against the shed.

Her cheerleading skirt was short, which probably made her legs look that much longer, and he had a hard time moving his eyes up to her face.

He knew he should walk slowly across the parking lot like he didn't care whether she waited for him or not, strutting even, but he couldn't make himself do that. He jogged.

"I didn't think you'd actually meet me."

"Of course." Her eyes got a little hooded as she gave him a flirty smile. Then, to his surprise, she pushed away from the shed and walked to him, not stopping until she put an arm around his neck and reached up, putting her lips on his.

He was shocked, too shocked to react, and she was gone before he could grab a hold of her and keep her pressed against him.

He figured his face probably showed how surprised he was, and that seemed to please her, because she got a coy smile on her face.

"I've missed you," she said, batting her eyes.

"I've missed you too. A lot." He took a step toward her, wanting to close the distance between them again.

But she put a hand up, and he stopped. "I don't have a whole lot of time."

"No. I know. I have to get back to...things," he finished lamely. He didn't want her to know that he was basically his brothers' babysitter.

"Of course. We're all busy. But," she gave him an assessing glance out from under her lowered eyelids, "I was hoping you would do a favor for me."

"Of course. Anything." He couldn't believe she was asking him to do something. He would move heaven and earth for her. Do anything she wanted.

"Super sweet of you." She smiled, with genuine joy, at least what he thought was genuine. Not that he knew that much about women. His mom had mentioned before that a woman needed to know how to work a man, but he knew Shanna wasn't that kind of girl.

"There are two of us who are teaching the cheerleading squad. I want you to distract Carrie, the other teacher."

"Distract her?"

"Sure. Whatever it takes." She gave him a look that made him feel like he should know what boys did to distract girls, but he really didn't have a clue.

"Right now?" he asked, figuring that if she wanted him to do it, he'd figure it out. Anything to get in her good graces.

"No, silly. When the football team comes around, I want to be able to talk to Chad, the captain. And I don't want Carrie interrupting us." She got that look in her eyes. The one that seemed a little calculating to Travis, but he thought he was wrong. It couldn't be calculating. It had to be admiring. That's it. She was admiring him.

"So you want me to talk to Carrie when the football team comes?"

"That's right. I want you, if you can," she put a hand on his arm, and the way she said "if you can" made him feel like he would be Superman if he could actually do what she was asking, "keep her away for me, because I have some very important things to discuss with Chad, and Carrie likes to interrupt our conversations and try to flirt with him, which is so annoying."

"Of course. Sounds to me like she has a crush on him, and she doesn't want anyone else to talk to him." That seemed like a pretty reasonable deduction, and he felt rather wise when Shanna nodded.

"That's exactly it. Those of us who have important business to discuss with the captain of the football team get thwarted by those of us who are more interested in flirting and doing, well, probably really bad things, if I know Carrie."

"Yeah. I know some girls like that. All right, I guess I'll make sure that she leaves you two alone, and I'll try to keep my virtue intact as well." He said that with a little bit of a smirk but wanting Shanna to know that he was all hers and he wouldn't be distracted by a girl who was flirting.

"Well, I want you to do whatever it takes. Even if you have to make...sacrifices."

His brows drew down just for a fraction of a second, because he thought she was saying that she really didn't care about his virtue. But that couldn't be it. Because surely the fact that she was trusting him with this assignment said that she liked him as much as he liked her. After all, she was talking to him. And she had chosen him out of all the boys in the school to do this with her.

"I'll make sure she's not bothering you."

"I knew I could count on you." Shanna took a step closer, put her hand on his cheek, and then tweaked his chin, almost like he was two instead of almost eighteen.

Maybe that's what girls did when they really liked someone, so he didn't allow it to bother him, but he leaned forward, wanting another kiss.

She reached a finger up and put it over his lips. "Not now. Someone might see." She lowered her eyes and her chin and whispered, "Later."

That one word gave his heart hope, and it blossomed in his chest and almost threatened to burst inside of him, he was so happy.

He watched as she walked away, her hips swinging, her tiny, minuscule skirt sliding from one side to the other, teasing him just a bit, like at any moment her underwear would peek out.

He knew he shouldn't watch her walk away, and at least he shouldn't be watching to see if that underwear actually did show, but...he did anyway.

Once she walked into the building, he walked away, whistling, taking up a post at the front of the community center and watching for the football team to come by.

It wasn't until later that night, when he was in bed, still smiling, that he realized he'd forgotten all about Ellen.

Chapter 17

Monday, Teagan didn't see Deuce all day. He had texted her and said that he'd be there that evening at Miss April's house, just to make sure that Gerald wasn't imposing. He said he had something he needed to talk to her about but that he had to travel to Fargo first thing Monday morning so he wouldn't be able to help her do any baking at her house.

Normally she and her sisters did all their baking on Monday, since Tuesday was their big farmers market down near Rockerton.

Often Deuce got up early, did his horse work, and came and helped her. A lot of times, she would sit with him in the evening while he worked on his family business. She often took notes and filled out spreadsheets for him, although she didn't do any of the actual IT work.

But it wasn't totally uncommon for him not to help on Monday, and she didn't think too much of it. Although she definitely was disappointed. After things had shifted between them on Sunday, she was eager to see him, to make sure that nothing had actually changed. Not in a bad way anyway.

She didn't want their friendship to be in jeopardy.

There was a small part of her, after he announced that he would not be seeing her on Monday, that wondered if he was backing out of the idea that they could be more. Or if he was uncomfortable with it and needed space. Or if whatever was happening was attributed to something that she had done wrong or something that he had changed his mind about.

By the time they got everything cooked and packed up ready to go to the farmers market and she was back at Miss April's house, she was more than a little worried.

Normally they texted a good bit during the day, but she had barely heard from him. He responded to her three texts with short answers, not rude, but not their usual conversations.

To make matters worse, Gerald waited for her on the porch, and it was impossible for her to get in the house without him following her in. And then, she didn't see either cat.

But as she went into Miss April's room, the true tragedy was that the parakeet was no longer in its cage.

That made her want to sit down and put her head in her hands and cry a little. Like crying would make things better.

"I thought you said you're going to change your clothes?" Gerald asked from his position on the couch, accusation in his tone like she had been lying to him.

"I realized that I have a really big evening ahead, and as much as I love to entertain the neighbors, I need to ask you to leave."

She prayed she wasn't being rude, but she just didn't think she could handle Gerald on top of everything else.

"Why is that? I waited all day for you to get home, because I wanted to spend time with you. And now this?"

"I just have a headache, and I can't take any more." She hated to be even a little bit weak, like she couldn't handle her life, but it was true. She couldn't handle her life. Not with Gerald in it.

"Listen, babe. This is where you lean on my shoulder, and we work through this together. Whatever is bothering you—"

"Nothing is bothering me. And I'm not your babe, and please don't call me that." That made her feel icky. Like he'd crossed a line that was clearly not his to cross.

She wanted to say it more strongly, everything, for him to leave, for him to not be so familiar with her, for him to not call her that, but she didn't want to take her stress out on him.

"Listen, babe, I mean, T." He put a hand on her shoulder.

It was all she could do not to knock it off. She took a step back, allowing it to fall, and ignored the fact that he had shortened her name without her permission.

"I'll open the door for you." She tried to smile, but she knew it was more like a grimace.

"Seriously, I'm not sure what your problem is, but we can work through this, I promise." He put a hand on the door as she tried to pull it open.

He didn't put any pressure on it, but she didn't like what that hand said. It made her panic just a little. She almost yanked the door open, but she didn't need to, since it opened from the other side as Deuce knocked and opened it at the same time.

"Well. You were just leaving," Deuce said, coming face-to-face with Gerald.

"No. I was working some things out with my T here, and you interrupted us. No one invited you in."

"I let him in. I want him here. And I want you to leave." There. Maybe she was rude, but it was the truth. She really did want him to leave. Like ten minutes ago. With Deuce standing there with his brows raised, Gerald didn't argue. That was even more annoying, that she could say she wanted him to leave, and he wouldn't listen to her, but all Deuce had to do was look at him, and he did whatever he wanted.

Annoying.

"I think it might be a good idea for you to stay at your house, unless Teagan invites you over. She works pretty hard, and I know she likes to relax in the evening, and entertaining guests is probably not high on her list of things to do. Especially since she's supposed to be housesitting and taking care of the pets, on top of her normal duties."

Gerald had a mulish look on his face, with his eyes narrowed. It was almost a glare as he looked back at her, a look that said "we'll talk more later," but she didn't meet his eyes and instead focused on Deuce's face, although Deuce watched Gerald.

Gerald left without saying anything more, and Teagan breathed a sigh of relief as Deuce closed the door behind him.

"Was he waiting on the porch when you got home?"

"Practically. He was on it before I had the door open and followed me in. It was disconcerting, especially since neither of the cats are here, and even worse than that, somehow the parakeet has gotten out of its cage!" She sighed, her back aching from the baking that she had done, and her feet tired, but she knew she couldn't relax until she had the animals taken care of.

"The parakeet got out of its cage?"

"Yes!"

"Was the door opened?"

"I didn't check. I just saw that the cage was empty, and that's when I decided that I was done being polite to Gerald, and I needed him to leave. I... I didn't want him to know. It's not that I'm not going to tell Miss April, of course I will. I just want to be able to tell her on my terms and not have him tattling on me, if that makes sense."

"Of course it makes sense. You're going to take responsibility for your actions, but he could shed those actions in a really bad light, if he so chooses. I don't trust him."

"I don't either," she said, grateful that Deuce said it first.

They stood, their eyes catching and holding.

It was the first that they'd seen each other since they'd talked about shifting their relationship, and it was like the idea both hit them both at once.

Whatever it was, it made Teagan pause, searching his face and feeling like there was a lot of things he wanted to tell her, that he was trying to find the words for. Or maybe he was just waiting. They had a parakeet and two cats loose in the house, and they needed to find hopefully all of them. Or maybe just one.

"Did you look in the room for it?" Deuce finally asked, ignoring all the other things that seemed to be heavy in the air between them and focusing on the one that was most important or at least needed their attention first.

"I didn't. I saw that the cage was empty and decided that the first thing I needed to do was get rid of Gerald. After all, if I'm going to find nothing but feet and feathers, I didn't want him looking over my shoulder as it happened."

"Smart move. Let's start in the bedroom. Was the door closed?"

"It was. I can't remember if it was closed tight..." She tried to think in her mind's eye if she had twisted the knob and pushed it open, but she'd been so irritated with Gerald that she honestly couldn't remember.

"Well, let's walk in, close the door behind us, and look in every nook and cranny we possibly can."

"That's a plan." It felt good to have him beside her, knowing that he was supporting her and that if she did lose the parakeet, he would be there when she had to explain to Miss April what happened.

They walked in the room, flipping the switch and looking around.

She didn't see any little yellow bird, and she couldn't keep her stomach from wanting to do jumping jacks. Even putting a hand over top of it didn't settle anything.

"I'm with you." Deuce's hand came down on her shoulder, and his eyes stared into hers as she looked over her shoulder at him.

"Thank you. I know it, but I appreciate your reassurance. For some reason, I needed it."

"Of course you needed it. No one wants to have to explain to someone that their cat ate their parakeet while they were supposed to be watching both animals."

"Thanks. You could've just stopped with the 'I'm with you,' and I would have been fine."

Her voice sounded wobbly, but they both laughed at her lame attempt at a joke.

"Is that bird poop on the comforter?" he asked, pointing toward the bed.

"It looks like it," Teagan said as she went closer.

Definitely it was, and it was still wet. She could see the shiny mess of it without having to touch it.

"So, it was out of the cage, and the cat didn't somehow get it out," she said, talking to herself but to Deuce as well.

But his eyes had gone from the bird poop up, and he pointed, tapping her shoulder.

"Right there."

Her eyes went up to the light and fan that was over the bed. The parakeet was perched on one blade.

"Oh, my goodness. There it is. It's alive!" She was so relieved, she couldn't help but laugh.

"Yeah, that's pretty awesome."

Then they were both silent for a minute, and Teagan voiced what Deuce surely was thinking.

"How are we going to catch it?"

"Is its wing clipped?"

"I don't know. I didn't think to ask. I never in a million years thought it would get out of its cage."

"I guess we'll see." He moved slowly to the bed, and she went around the end and moved carefully to the other side. The fan was almost directly in the middle, but the parakeet was sitting on a blade that was closer to Deuce's side.

"I'll talk, and maybe I can get it to look at me, and you can sneak up behind it."

"Good idea. Maybe you can move your arm slowly, give it something to look at."

"Okay, parakeet. I forget what Miss April said your name was, or maybe she didn't tell me? I'm sorry. It must be terrible being taken care of by someone who doesn't even know your name." She spoke silliness to it, moving her hand, seeing that the bird was indeed watching her.

Deuce's hand came up, swiping at the feet but grabbing the entire body in his palm.

"Got it!" he said.

"Wow. I would never in a million years have thought we would have caught it on the first try."

"We?" Deuce raised his eyebrows at her.

"I was the distraction," she said, holding her arms out in front of her, palms up.

"I know. I'm teasing. I don't know what it was, but I didn't think we were going to get it on the first try either. I kind of pictured us going down to the hardware store and asking for a fishing net and trying to get it that way."

"Oh. That's a good idea. I didn't even think about that."

"Well, we didn't need it, so that's a good thing."

She walked around the end of the bed while he turned toward the cage.

"The door's open. I wonder if it got jostled somehow? Did Miss April say anything about moving it?"

"No. If she kept it somewhere else, she didn't tell me. But... I guess maybe she could have moved it out of wherever she normally kept it to keep the cats away from it while she was gone."

"When you tell her about it, you can ask if maybe she did move it."

"Yes. I'm definitely telling her. I couldn't keep something like this away from her, but it's nice that I can tell her that the parakeet is fine and that everything is okay." She chewed on her lip. "As long as we can find both cats."

"I don't see any reason why we shouldn't be able to."

"Cordilia always seems to go missing. He makes me nervous."

"He must have a hiding spot that we haven't found yet. Because he was somewhere yesterday, and he just appeared, without us having been outside after we looked for him."

"That's true. He couldn't have gone in or out because we didn't."

"We might never figure out where he's hiding, but I bet it's somewhere obvious."

"Maybe."

He closed the parakeet's cage door behind him while Teagan filled up the water and checked the food.

"That was enough excitement for one day, I think," she said.

He laughed, as she expected him to, and after checking the cage one more time, they both walked out.

The air felt heavy as they walked into the kitchen, and she considered asking him what the issue was, but she figured they ought to find the cats first. That would be a distraction if they needed to talk about something serious. Even though she wanted to get whatever was between them out of the way. She wasn't used to having this feeling of tension and expectation between them. Usually their relationship felt easy, something comfortable to slip into even when the rest of the world was going crazy. But it didn't feel like that to her today.

"Here's one of our cats," Deuce said, and he was already kneeling as she turned to look. Sure enough, Elizabeth brushed up against his knee.

"That's great. Now all we have to do is find Cordilia."

"You didn't see him this morning?"

"No. It was early when I left, not quite five, and I fed and watered them, but I didn't see him at all."

"You had a big day baking. I'm sorry I wasn't around to help."

"A big day today, and my sisters are going to the farmers market in Rockerton tomorrow, but they wanted me to bake some things and take it to a big community yard sale that's going on in Briarwood."

"That's tomorrow?"

"Yeah. It's yard sale Tuesday. A big thing they do every year. We were there last year and sold out within the first hour, remember? It's not as big as the farmers market for us over the course of the year, of course, but big enough that we decided I would go ahead and work on it tomorrow."

"I can help you. I'll get up early and do my horses. I actually have the two that the guys on the Sweet Briar Ranch asked me to do, and I'd like to get those done...because of something I need to talk to you about."

"I knew there was something on your mind."

"It's funny how you can tell that."

"Yeah," she said and didn't say anything else. She didn't know whether it was her intuition that was kicking in, or whether it was just her being afraid. He would call it her intuition, but it always surprised him because he didn't seem to be able to read people's emotions the way she could.

Or maybe it wasn't an emotion as much as it was that she just looked at him and knew.

Maybe that really was intuition.

She called Cordilia, imitating what Miss April had done. Although, Miss April calling her hadn't made her come, either.

Crawling around on her hands and knees, she looked under the couch and the chairs in the living room, under the dining room table, and in the bathroom behind the toilet. She even looked in the shower stall, but no cat.

Finally, she went into the kitchen and sat down on the floor, dejected. Where in the world could he be?

"I assume he wasn't in any of the bedrooms, because the doors were closed," she said, leaning against the cupboard while Deuce, carrying Elizabeth, slid down the refrigerator and sat on the floor with her, their feet stretching out in front of them as they faced each other.

"Well, one out of two isn't bad."

"Two out of three, really."

"You're right. That's even better."

"I guess I don't need to panic. I couldn't find him yesterday, and he ended up showing up. As long as Gerald…"

"He doesn't have a key. And the door was locked. Right?"

She thought back. She was pretty sure it had been. She hadn't left it unlocked anyway, but she couldn't remember whether it clicked or not when she used her key that evening because Gerald had appeared at her elbow, and she had wished that she had done things a little faster so she could have gotten in before he caught her.

"I'm pretty sure it was. I used the key to unlock the door, but I can't remember if it clicked or not."

"Meow."

"What was that?" Deuce asked, tilting his head.

Teagan tilted hers as well and listened intently. It had sounded like a cat.

Teagan looked around. It was obviously a cat meowing, but she couldn't tell where the sound was coming from.

It had sounded like it was coming from behind her.

She twisted, looking up at the counter. "Am I missing something on the counter?"

"I think it might be coming from the cupboard."

Deuce had no sooner said that than the cupboard door wiggled, and a little nose stuck out, right beside her elbow.

"Oh, my goodness. He's been in the cupboard!" Teagan exclaimed, but in a soft voice so she didn't scare the cat.

He sat there for a moment, just his nose pushing the cupboard door open, before he seemed to think that it was safe to come out, or maybe he realized he had been discovered.

Either way, he pushed the cupboard door open with his face and slipped out.

"The door doesn't shut quite tight. He must have figured out he can push it open… I wonder if Miss April realizes he's been hanging out in there?"

"If she did, she didn't mention it to me when she was telling me about it." Teagan ran a hand down Cordilia's sleek fur. "You'd think it's something she would have thought to mention."

"Maybe it slipped her mind. She was pretty excited about her trip."

Teagan smiled and nodded. That was true. Miss April had been super thrilled to be going to Italy. "I guess I can't blame her. There's a lot of things to remember when you're packing for a trip like that and being gone for three weeks. If she forgot, it's totally understandable."

"Well, I know where I'm looking the next time we can't find him. First."

"And the parakeet. If it gets out again, I'm going to think about the ceiling fan first."

"Wow, the things the animals teach us." Deuce grinned. And Teagan shared a smile with him. It almost felt a little bit like the animals were ruling the roost around Miss April's house, but she didn't mind. As long as everything had turned out well, which she felt it had.

They sat, with Deuce petting Elizabeth and Teagan petting Cordilia, before Teagan decided she might as well start a conversation she didn't want to have. At least she was sitting down for it.

"So… You said there was something you wanted to talk to me about?"

"Yeah, about that." Deuce rubbed the bridge of his nose. A sure sign he was not comfortable. It was one of his tells, and Teagan hid a smile. She knew him so well. If he was rubbing the bridge of his nose, he was about to say something he really didn't want to.

Then she remembered it could be about her, and her smile faded and her stomach erupted with what felt like bubbly glue.

She focused on petting the cat, feeling the soothing slide of his fur under the palm of her hand.

"My parents want me to move to Fargo and help with the business there." He didn't pull any punches and threw it out there in one sentence.

"Is that it?" she asked, hardly daring to believe that it wasn't about them and their relationship.

"I felt like it was really bad timing because of what you and I have been talking about."

All right. That was what she was afraid of. She decided she would head it off. "That's fine. We don't have to change anything now. How long do they want you out there? Two months? Three months? We'll just wait until you come back before we make any changes."

"Two years."

Her hand froze, and her head jerked up.

"Two *years*?" she asked, emphasizing "years."

She knew she hadn't misheard, because he nodded his head up and down slowly.

"Years. Two."

"I know you feel like you owe your parents. That they provided a job for you and a business for you to step into. And you love what you do with the horses, and you wouldn't be able to do that without them." She knew all that. They'd talked about that before. Not endlessly, but he'd mentioned it more than once. He really did love his parents and appreciate that they'd opened up positions in their company and made them suit the interests and abilities of their children.

That he'd been able to have a job where he could work in the evening and still train horses during the day.

"What about your horses?"

"I have four I'm training now, and they won't be finished by the time my parents told me to leave. I haven't decided what I'm doing, but beyond that, I'm in a good spot. I'll have to figure a few things out, but it can be done."

She knew once he had them started well, he could be back on the weekends and finish them up. He didn't say that, but she read between the lines that that might be what he was thinking about.

"What do they need from you?" She didn't want to ask that question. She didn't want to hear what his parents needed. She wanted this all to go away. She would be losing her best friend, and it was obvious to her that anything that they had thought that they might start needed to be put on hold.

"They want me to take the supervisor position of the warehouse in Fargo. It's not doing well, and it's all hands on deck to try to save it." He explained a little more, and she got the gist of what he was saying and what they wanted him to do. "Obviously, I can come home on the weekends like they often do. But I'd be leaving Sunday afternoon to go back."

He paused, and she thought this might be where the relationship thing was coming in, but not yet.

"They said if I did this for two years, they would put my name on the deed of the farm."

She gasped a little, knowing what that meant to him. It was his dream to have a ranch, but they were expensive, and not many people had the money to be able to buy one, and even if they did have the money to put down, they often had to have a second or third job because most of the time the money that they made from ranching wasn't enough to make the payments and keep the mortgage current. In a good year, sure, but there were just as many bad years as good, and that wasn't something a person could control.

"I know you know what that means to me."

He didn't need to say that, but she nodded. She knew exactly what it meant to him.

"They want you that bad?"

He shrugged. "I guess they've had people who haven't been upright and honest with them. Several in a row if I understand them correctly. They want to circle the wagons, so to speak, and put the family in charge until they have it up and running, and I assume, although they hadn't said yet, that I would be putting some safeguards in place to make sure that the next people that they have aren't able to get away with things that the last people have."

She knew that the IT work was often his. It was a lot of times things that he could do from home and things he did in the evening.

But this sounded a little more complicated, and considering that the warehouse was in Fargo, it would be different than the work he had done with the Sweet Water warehouse. Where, if he needed to make a trip to the warehouse and do a few things, it wasn't a big deal. Fargo was a completely different story.

"Did you tell them you would do it?" She wasn't sure why she asked that question. She was pretty sure he was going to say yes, and he probably did so immediately.

"I told them I owed them, and I knew it. I also told them that I wanted to talk to you."

"Me?"

He nodded. "I... I can't imagine leaving you for two years. We've...been together all of our lives. Separated for a few nights, but I've never gone more than a week without seeing you."

"I know." She hated the thought, but she also knew that was life sometimes. "Maybe that was what the ladies were talking about, or maybe that was why you had that premonition, remember? When you said what if we're not together forever? And how you were thinking about that? Maybe this is why."

"Because we're going to be separated?"

"Yeah. I mean, Fargo isn't days away, but it's too far to drive every day. And it sounds to me like you're going to be working pretty hard."

"Yeah. I will be."

Silence fell in the kitchen, with just the purring of Cordilia on her lap reaching her ears to break it.

She hadn't known that this would happen, but she had known that someday something might happen that would pull them apart.

It was life. She had to face it head-on, the same way she had to face anything else.

"How soon do they want you?"

"They gave me two weeks."

Two weeks. That was all they had together. Before he left for two years.

Not that she wouldn't see him in those two years, but they would almost certainly drift apart.

"I didn't mean to make everything all depressed tonight."

"Well, you didn't. It's a sad thing, but it's a life thing." She shrugged her shoulders. "If you aren't leaving yet and have time, I have to go out in the morning and make soup for the big yard sale."

"You and I went together last year, and we sold out within an hour."

"Yeah. We could have taken ten times as much as what we did and made a killing."

"Of course you don't want to miss that."

"Right. So, unless you're going to be busy with your horses, I'd love to have you with me in the morning."

"I'll be there. I... I'm not looking forward to this, but I know I have to do it. I couldn't turn my parents down. I just... I just hate the idea that it's going to come between you and me."

"Well, it's not going to change our friendship. It's just something we have to deal with."

"Two years seems like an eternity."

"By the time you're seventy, it'll feel like a blink." She grinned a little, because the idea of being seventy years old was almost inconceivable when a person was in their early thirties.

She supposed, though, time flew by faster and faster the older a person got. That had been true in her life anyway. She couldn't believe she was thirty. It felt like just yesterday that she had graduated from high school.

"All right, what do you have ready for supper?"

"Nothing. Normally I burn a batch or at least char something a little, and I get to take something home, but today I didn't even undercook anything."

"You had a perfect day?"

"I guess. Which is good, but it means a hungry night."

"How about I take you to the diner? Jane's trying out a new soup for her class this coming Sunday, and I've heard it's been popular. I bet if we go right now, she won't have sold out yet."

"All right. Sounds good. And maybe we can make an agreement that we'll not talk about anything depressing tonight. Tomorrow will be soon enough."

He looked like he wanted to argue, and she couldn't imagine why. Surely he didn't want to talk about anything that would make him sad any more than what she did.

But after a short pause, he nodded decisively. "Deal. Nothing depressing tonight."

He held his hand out, and she clasped it, with both of them leaning back and standing up together.

They'd done it a million times, and there was nothing different about this time, other than she knew that a separation was looming, and she didn't like it. Not one bit.

Chapter 18

"Aunt Charlene said that we should make a deal with Mr. Marshall and the other guys who take lessons from my mom."

Sorrell sat on the steps outside the back door of the diner. Merritt, her younger sister, had a jump rope she was idly swinging and jumping over.

Her best friend, Toni, sat beside her.

"Your Aunt Charlene is known as a matchmaker," Toni said, sounding thoughtful. Of course, Toni always sounded thoughtful. Being that she was being raised by a single mom, and it made her life hard, and she wasn't used to things being handed to her. She was used to working, and that suited Sorrell just fine. Since Sorrell was used to working for things too. Plus, she had a little sister to look after, which Toni didn't.

"I don't think she's trying to match us up with anyone. We're too little," Sorrell said.

"Not us, the old men. They're trying to find a lady."

"I know. But they're also trying to do TikTok. I don't think Aunt Charlene wanted us to match anybody up. She said we should switch out what we know with what we don't know."

"I think they would appreciate us matching them up. They need a lady, and we need someone for our moms. That would be a fair trade."

"But we don't know anything about matching adults. Plus, they won't listen to us about that. But they will listen to us about TikTok. After all, we know everything there is to know about that."

That might have been a big statement, but she felt pretty confident in her ability to navigate social media. She heard adults saying that it wasn't safe and that she should be careful, and she listened. She was careful, she wasn't going to let anyone take advantage of her, but she also knew that there was money to be made, and she wasn't about to let everyone else make that money. Some of it was going to be hers.

And her friends. Of course she would share, because they helped her with everything.

"Maybe we could do both."

Toni wasn't giving up the idea of matchmaking, and Sorrell had learned from experience that when Toni got an idea, it was usually pretty good.

She put the hair tie that she had been wrapping around her fingers back on her wrist and turned to her friend. "You have a plan?"

"Nothing beyond talking to them and seeing if we can hash something out. Unless of course, we really want to match them up, and then I think we can do what we are thinking about doing with our moms, and that is tie them up together."

"I think we would get in trouble if we did that," Merritt injected into their conversation.

Merritt was the one who never wanted to take any risk. Sorrell had told her over and over again that if she wanted to get anywhere in life, sometimes she had to close her eyes and just jump.

Merritt didn't close her eyes and jump anywhere. She always jumped with her eyes wide open and usually with both hands holding tight to Sorrell.

Sorrell didn't mind, because that's what big sisters were for.

"That's a last resort. If we can think of something else, we won't do it. But if that's the only thing that's going to work, then we have to take a risk." Sorrell tried to make the words sound reasonable, and beside her, Toni nodded. Merritt still didn't look interested. She had that look on her face, that Merritt got sometimes when she was being stubborn. And Sorrell had never met anyone who could be more stubborn than Merritt.

"We won't know until we talk to them," Toni said.

"But we shouldn't just go talk to them without a plan. We have to have an idea."

"We're pretty decent with TikTok. It won't be hard." Toni shrugged her shoulders like it was no big deal.

"But what are they gonna do? How are they going to find us a man to match our moms up with? And how do we know that they'll keep their word?"

"We'll make them pinky promise," Merritt said.

Sorrell pressed her lips together and gave her sister a disgusted glance. "Adults don't do pinky promise, silly."

"Sometimes old men do," Toni said, chewing on her fingernail.

Sorrell had told Toni multiple times that she shouldn't bite her fingernails, but it was a habit that Toni hadn't been able to break.

Sometimes you had to love somebody even though they had bad habits. That's what her mom said anyway.

"Okay. I'm not going to argue about that, because you could be right. But we don't know if these old men are the kind of old men who pinky promise or not."

"What old men are you talking about?" A gruff voice came from beside the building as Mr. Marshall's face appeared.

He was followed by Mr. Blaze and Mr. Junior, and Sorrell was half annoyed and half embarrassed at being caught talking about them.

"You. They were talking about you," Merritt said, with the kind of honesty that only a little sister had.

Sorrell rolled her eyes at Toni but then looked back at the old men, who didn't seem angry that they had been talking about them.

"I do pinky promise. What about you guys?" Mr. Marshall said, looking back at Mr. Blaze and Mr. Junior.

"What's a pinky promise?" Mr. Blaze asked.

"It's when you promise, and then you shake on it, only you shake with your pinky finger, because that means more than a regular handshake." Merritt was the top of her class in school, but sometimes people who were book smart didn't really know anything worthwhile.

Merritt was book smart, but she had absolutely no brain when it came to manipulating people.

But the old men again didn't seem upset. They talked among themselves about whether or not they ever pinky promised.

Two out of the three hadn't.

Sorrell looked at Toni with her brows raised, almost an I told you so kind of glance. These men were not going to be people that they could work with on this strength of a promise.

Too many times, adults had lied to them both. They had agreed hundreds of times when they talked about it before that you couldn't trust adults. Except for their moms.

"I've never broken a pinky promise," Mr. Marshall said casually.

Sorrell wasn't sure whether to believe him or not, but Toni looked at him as though she was inclined to do so.

"Really? Never?"

He shook his head.

Sorrell was still hesitant. But her mom trusted him. And that said a lot to Sorrell. Usually her mom had really good judgment. Except, her mom said she hadn't had such great judgment with her dad.

But she said that when someone made mistakes, once they knew what they were, they could learn from them and get wiser. So that's what she tried to do.

That's really all her mom ever said about her dad, which was too bad, because Sorrell would like to know more.

"How do we know we can trust you to keep a pinky promise?" Sorrell asked, crossing her arms over her chest and looking Mr. Marshall right in the eye.

"The same way I know I can trust you," Mr. Marshall said, crossing his own arms over top of his chest, then uncrossing them, and leaning back on his cane.

Sorrell waited, but he didn't explain how he knew he could trust her, so she figured she had to ask. "And what is that?"

"Because I trust your mom. And she trusts you. So I will too."

He had her there. She had been thinking along the same lines.

"One minute." She motioned to Merritt to come closer, then she put one arm around Toni and one arm around Merritt and bent their heads together.

"What you think?" she whispered.

"He's right. Mom trusts him," Merritt said without hesitation.

"I know. What do you think, Toni?"

"What's the worst that is going to happen if he doesn't do what he says?"

That was a good point. Sorrell thought about that for a minute. "It's not like we're going to pay them anything. We're just trading services. The worst that will happen is that he'll learn to use TikTok, and we won't get any man for our moms."

"You need to specify that you want two men. One for your mom, and one for mine. None of that sister wives thing."

Sorrell wrinkled up her nose and stuck her finger in her mouth, making a gag motion. "Of course not. That's gross." She pulled her finger back out of her mouth. "I'll make sure. Two men."

"Okay. I say we trust them. And we'll make them all pinky promise."

Sorrell nodded in agreement. "And I know Mom said that we have to respect our elders, but maybe we can just tell them that we're going to hide their canes if they lie to us."

"We can't hide their canes. That's not nice, and Mom said we have to do unto others as we would have them do unto us. Even if they're not nice to us. In fact, Mom says especially if they're not nice to us." Merritt's whispered voice got a little heated at the end, and she tried to pull away and cross her arms over her chest, but Sorrell took a glance at the men and pulled her in closer.

"All right. You're right, Merritt. Okay. We won't hide their canes." She still thought hiding their canes was a really good idea, but she didn't want Merritt to get mad. Sometimes when Merritt got mad, she tattled on them, and if her mom found out that she suggested hiding the men's canes, she'd probably have to do the dishes for a month and she'd never find a man for her mom.

Merritt's face said that she knew it, but she also wanted to be in the group, so she knew she wouldn't tattle unless there was a good reason.

"All right. This is what we'll do. We'll trust them, telling them that we'll teach them how to use TikTok, a little bit at a time. Maybe...stretch it out to six lessons. In the meantime, we'll see what they come up with in the men department. If they don't show, we'll cut off the TikTok lessons." She looked at both girls' faces, with her brows raised.

Toni nodded immediately, and her eyes shifted to Merritt. Merritt nodded too, and she said, "That's okay. We don't have to teach them TikTok if they don't do what they say."

"We should know, if we give them three weeks, at one lesson a week, then three lessons in, we should have a good idea whether or not they're going to cough up a man or not."

"And if they come up with some good men," Sorrell looked at both girls, letting them know that she had a really good idea, before she said, "then we can go to Miss Charlene and we can find a woman for them."

She was pretty proud of herself, thinking that was a really great idea. And she was a little disappointed when it took the other girls several long seconds before they saw the beauty in her idea, and sly smiles graced their faces.

"Deal?" she asked, holding her hand out in the middle space between their bodies.

Both of them leaned back a little, and they put their hands on top of hers, and they both said, "Deal," at the same time.

Sorrell smiled at her friend and her sister. It was nice to have a group who looked out for each other.

She kept her mouth closed, her lips pressed together, but she couldn't contain her smile as she leaned out, looked over at Mr. Marshall, and said, "This is what we're going to do."

Chapter 19

Teagan held Minnie on one hip, stirring a pot of soup with one hand while leaning over the counter and trying to tap her phone with one of the fingers of the hand that was holding up Minnie, to see how much time was left on the timer.

So far, it had been the kind of morning where everything that could go wrong had. With bells on.

Figures it would be the morning that her sisters were gone. Two of them had gone to the farmers market, and the other had gone to a convention. It was a big convention, and they were hoping that she would learn some new techniques for growing long-day plants in a greenhouse to extend the growing season some on both ends.

In the meantime, Teagan had thought it was going to be easy to cook up a batch of soup and throw a few loaves of bread that she had set out at midnight to rise in the oven. So she'd have bread and soup and the vegetables that they packed the night before.

It had turned out to be anything but easy, when the tractor wouldn't start and she was unable to feed the stock.

Her sisters had left earlier, and she had gone out to feed at the same time.

Thankfully, Deuce had come, although he had Minnie in tow.

She never minded watching Minnie, who was always a sweetheart, although this early in the morning, all she wanted was to hold her blanket, suck her thumb, and have Teagan hold her.

It wouldn't have been so hard if she hadn't been trying to cook soup and make sure she didn't burn the bread at the same time.

Still, Deuce had gone out to see if he could fix the tractor and get it working, and if not, figure out a way to feed the stock in the meantime.

She would take Deuce, even if it meant she had to hold Minnie. After all, she had no idea how to fix the tractor.

Still, she got the soup thrown together, and once it came to a low simmer, she would call it good.

Trying to remember if she put everything in, in the hustle and bustle of holding Minnie and making sure the baby bag was somewhere where she wouldn't trip over it, and also getting the first batch of bread out and the next batch in and realizing that she had gotten the wrong blanket when Minnie threw it on the floor.

She was going over everything in her mind when Deuce walked in the door.

"They're fed. I got it to start. It looked like a loose wire, but I also had it on the charger, so you might need a new battery. I didn't take the time to completely diagnose it this morning. But I can once we get home. I just knew you were in a hurry."

"I really appreciate it," she said gratefully.

"I didn't get a chance to ask if you saw the parakeet and both cats this morning?"

"The parakeet was in its cage, the door was closed, both cats were there, although I had to open the cupboard door to see Cordilia, but now that I know where he stays, it wasn't hard. There's food, water, and the door is closed and locked." She ticked everything off in her head as she spoke to Deuce.

"Sounds like you have everything under control."

"It might sound that way, but it doesn't feel that way. I feel like I'm forgetting something."

"Well, I'm here. Let me take Minnie, and if you have stuff for me to carry out to the car, I'll happily do it."

"It's time for me to take the bread out of the oven. I'll need a few minutes for it to cool down, but then once I wrap it and put the soup in the containers, we're ready to go." She gave Minnie a glance. "Did you change her diaper?"

"No, I ran out the door with her, and you and I might have passed her off like a football as I was on my way down the walk."

"Poor Minnie," she said softly.

She closed her mouth over anything more. She wanted to ask Deuce about how the situation was going with Minnie's parents, but she didn't want to do it in front of Minnie, and it seemed like there were so many other things to talk about when they finally got alone, or maybe it was just her having to go through all the feelings that she wasn't used to feeling.

As it was, she had a hard time looking at Deuce and thinking friend. She had wanted to grab a hold of his hand and hug him when he walked in.

Despite the crazy morning and the frenzy of not being able to get everything done, she wanted to lean into him.

It was a new feeling that she wasn't used to. Normally she'd always been happy standing beside him. This desire to touch him was different.

Thirty minutes later, they had the soup in quart containers in three different coolers, and the bread wrapped and packed in the back of the pickup, along with the vegetables.

"I think we're actually going to be early," she said as Deuce pulled out of the driveway.

"No way," he said, glancing at the console and the time. She could see the wheels turning in his head as he estimated how long it would take to get there. "I think you're right."

"I guess we should have problems like that every day. It makes us go faster." She laughed.

"Maybe we just work well together under pressure."

"That's your abilities coming out, then, because I have a tendency to do worse under pressure. I can't stand it."

And that was true. She hated it whenever everything depended on her, and she had to have things turn out perfectly. It seemed like the harder she tried to make things perfect, the worse they turned out.

Deuce was always a calming influence on her and helped her relax.

He chatted easily the rest of the way there, telling her a story about something his sister did that was funny, and they were laughing by the time they got to the yard sale, and she wasn't even thinking about whether or not they were late.

They were able to park behind their assigned stall and unload their car. One of them holding Minnie and working with one hand, but they traded off, so neither one of them had to hold her the whole time, which Teagan appreciated because her arm got tired.

She didn't know how some of the moms who had two or three children actually did it all.

She didn't think about that too much, although she did spare a glance for the lady on her right who had four children who were "helping" her.

They had barely gotten their table set up with the quarts of soup on it when people started stopping.

Teagan stopped unloading the car to wait on customers while Deuce set up the rest of the vegetables, setting out napkins and plastic spoons as well as her cashbox and the tape she would use to tape prices down on the table.

They were still setting up ten minutes later when her first customer came back.

"I just wanted you to know that the soup is very bland." The older lady seemed kindly, and Teagan assumed she was trying to help.

"Bland?" she said, running back in her head, trying to think of what she had done. At least it wasn't scorched. She had put spices in, and the onion she had cooked the night before. Along with some garlic... Salt. She hadn't put any salt in.

"Salt?" Teagan asked as she slapped her forehead and the lady nodded. "I know I forgot to put the salt in."

"Hang on." Deuce slipped around the table as Teagan apologized to the lady and offered her her money back.

"No. I'm actually on a low-sodium diet, and this is probably really good for me, but I just wanted you to know so that you're not selling this to other customers and having people come and complain."

Teagan thanked her again, regretfully told the next lady in line that she wasn't selling any more soup, and sold a loaf of bread and two heads of lettuce and a ten-pound bag of potatoes before Deuce came back.

He had a container of salt in one hand and a box of baggies in the other.

"I'll pour a teaspoon of salt in each baggie, then we'll tape them onto the containers of soup and tell people we're selling them with 'add your own salt,' just in case their doctors have advised them to cut back on sodium."

"You're brilliant, and you're a lifesaver," Teagan said, closing her eyes for a moment and just being so thankful that Deuce was there to look out for her.

She didn't really think about it, but she put her free arm around him and laid her head on his chest.

If he hesitated, she couldn't tell. It seemed like his arm came right around her, and he leaned his head down on hers.

"I don't think I'm a lifesaver so much as we just work well together. But I think we also already had that conversation this morning, and I might have said those exact same words."

"You might have. And you are right."

"Excuse me. I'm next." A man's voice interrupted them, and Teagan pulled back. She glanced up at Deuce, who was looking down at her, and they shared a second quick look before she turned to the man.

He bought soup, and Deuce taped salt to the top of it before the man walked away.

He took Minnie from her, and they worked on getting a little bit of salt in each baggie and taping it to each container of soup while she continued to take care of the customers who were standing in line.

By the time eleven o'clock rolled around, her feet were aching, her back hurt, and customers had been coming nonstop. Which was a good thing, because they were sold out of onions and lettuce and only had twenty pounds of potatoes left and three containers of soup. The loaves of bread had been the first thing to go, and Teagan had texted one of her sisters saying to make a note that the bread was popular, and they should bring more next year.

"Excuse me, are you the people who were selling the soup?" a customer said as Teagan had turned to check on Minnie.

She saw her sitting on the cooler, holding her cup and her blanket.

She'd been up early and was probably more than ready for a nap, even though it was early for her.

Teagan turned around. "That's us."

"I'd like four quarts, please. And I understand that I need to get salt to go along with it?"

"Yes. We have salt in baggies to go along with it, in case your doctor has put you on a salt-restricted diet."

"That was brilliant marketing. I don't know who thought of that idea, but several other vendors down the way have been talking about how they should do that next time."

"Thanks. It was something we just thought of today." And boy was that the truth. "Although I only have three quarts left."

The man wanted what was left and also asked for potatoes. Deuce passed them over as she gave him napkins for people who had come back to ask for them. And then he handed her a box to put the containers of soup in while she passed him their last bag of spinach for the next customer in line that he was waiting on.

The man paid with a fifty-dollar bill, and she said, "Can you give me a five and four ones please?" Since Deuce was standing directly in front of the cashbox.

He grabbed it out without saying anything and took the bag of spinach she handed him.

"You two work really well together. More married couples should work together like you do. Seems like people get married, and then all they can do is fight and try to get away from each other." The man chuckled.

"Aw, we're not—"

"Thanks."

Teagan looked at Deuce. Thanks? What was he thinking?

He just grinned at her and winked.

She shook her head, handed the man his change, and looked back to check on Minnie again.

Minnie had stood, picking up her blanket and walking over to Teagan, with her arms up.

"I think it's about time for us to call it a day. That man just cleaned us out of soup, and if we can sell those last potatoes, we're in good shape." She glanced at Deuce. "I'll set them on the table at a reduced price while we start packing up the car."

"You sit down with Minnie on your lap, and I'll get the car packed up."

Teagan appreciated that. She'd been up late the night before, talking to her sister about the different classes being offered at the conference and which ones she should attend. They'd been on a conference call, and it had gone until late in the night.

She shouldn't have been up so late, knowing that the day was going to be so busy. But it seemed like she could always count on Deuce to take care of her, and she appreciated that.

She sank gratefully into the chair, after putting out the potatoes and a special price on a fluorescent piece of paper, sure to draw the eye.

Sure enough, within five minutes they had sold out and took their table down so people would stop asking if they had anything left.

By the time they had the car loaded, Minnie's eyes drooped, and she didn't even protest when Teagan changed her diaper and put her in her car seat.

"She's going to sleep the whole way home," she said softly.

Deuce nodded. "You look tired, too."

"I guess I am. The last few days have been kind of stressful."

"I'm sorry. I'm part of the reason that they have."

"It's not your fault. But it is sad to think of you leaving."

"It's hard for me too. I... I feel like I'm choosing my parents over you. I hate that."

"That's what I want you to do. You and I both know that you owe them, and... I like to think our friendship is strong enough to weather a separation like that."

That wasn't the issue that she was thinking about, and she figured they both knew it. She knew their friendship was strong enough. She knew they'd find ways to get together. It was the idea that they had been thinking about more, and that was going to have to be tabled.

But neither of them said what they both were thinking.

"But it made me appreciate today more. Just being able to be with you. You know how you were saying that we take things for granted. That was true, and I kept thinking today how much I appreciate the things you've done. And how much it was going to stink when I had to do them all by myself."

"You'll be fine," he said, then his face became serious. "Except, I don't like the idea of you having all that work to do alone. I like to know that I'm here to help you."

"I like to know that, too."

"And of course, you've always repaid the favor and been there when I needed you."

She nodded, and they were quiet. Not really saying anything more, just lost in their own thoughts.

Chapter 20

"You're quiet," Zaylee said, later that afternoon as Teagan sat in the living room, adding up everything that she had sold at the yard sale.

Minnie had fallen asleep on the way home and was still sleeping upstairs in her pack and play.

Teagan had offered to keep her so that Deuce could go and work with his horses.

They hadn't talked about Minnie or her parents, but that was one of the things she wanted to talk to Deuce about. She just…didn't want to get into too many serious subjects, because there were too many things she really didn't want to talk about.

"I know," she said softly, knowing that Zaylee would question her more but not knowing how to head that off.

"Want to talk about it?"

"I don't know that there's anything I can say."

"This has to do with Deuce leaving?"

"How did you hear about that?" she asked, narrowing her eyes.

"Small town, remember?"

"I remember. I guess I just haven't processed it yet, and I'm not ready for the world to know."

"Well, ready or not, the world knows, at least the Sweet Water part of the world anyway." They shared a smile while Zaylee sat down on the chair opposite of Teagan, and Teagan tapped the pencil in her lap.

"So what's the issue?" Zaylee said.

"That's a long time to be away from someone."

"You want to go with him?" she asked, and her words sounded so simple they made Teagan's head jerk up.

"You don't follow your friend across the state and just hang out with them in a different city. What would you guys do without me anyway?"

"First of all, we'd miss you, but that's life, isn't it? People leave. And we'll fill your spot with someone else, or we'll all just pitch in and take your share."

"I would never do that to you guys."

"When are you two going to see that there is more to your relationship than just friendship? That you guys are perfect for each other?"

"You know, it's funny you should say something." Did she really want to go into this? Did she want to talk to her sister about it? She wanted advice, but she didn't want someone who was just going to tell her that she ought to do whatever that person wanted her to do. She wanted good advice, not advice that suited the other person. "Would you tell me something honestly?"

"Have I ever been anything but honest with you?" Zaylee asked gently.

"No. You haven't."

"I didn't think so. Now, what is it?"

"Deuce and I were actually talking about whether we wanted to...be more in our relationship."

"Of course you do. What's the hang-up?"

"Well, he kind of phrased it in a way that said that's what everybody expects of us, so if we do it, people will leave us alone rather than constantly being in our faces about needing to be more. He used the example of Brooklyn and Cormac. He said if they would just kiss and make up, people would stop pushing them together. It's because it's so much fun to see the antagonism between them that people keep doing it."

"I see."

"What do you see?"

"He wanted to be more, not based on his feelings for you, but based on what everybody else in the town wanted."

"Well, that's kind of what I just said."

"And that hurt your feelings."

"He did not—" Teagan cut her sentence off. Was that what the problem was? Was she nursing hurt feelings because Deuce hadn't actually said to her that he had feelings for her, he had just said that he wanted to try to be more because it was something everyone else expected?

"I think I know that he wanted to do it himself though. Maybe he didn't say that exactly, but that was the impression I got." She spoke slowly, wanting to make sure that her words were true before she put them out in the air.

"And that is why you're resisting? Because you're unsure about how he felt?"

"I think we're both unsure about how we feel. I think the big problem between us was that we were afraid that if we try to do something more, and it didn't last, that it would make things awkward between us and it would ruin our friendship. Neither one of us wanted that."

"Of course not. You guys have the best friendship of anyone I've ever seen. But so many times a good friendship makes an even better marriage."

"I guess that's true. But how do you slip from friendship into more?"

"I don't think there's any slip into it. You have to decide that the risk is worth it. All good things come with risk. You can't expect to have things happen to you without risking other things."

Teagan thought about that for a little bit, and Zaylee continued. "It's like with our business. When we spend a bunch of money on seed, or on improvements to our rowhouses, or when we decide to branch out into something new, everything that we do carries a risk that people aren't going to like it, aren't going to buy it, or that it's not going to work out. We can't just sell things without taking a risk first. You know that."

She did. And ranching was even harder, because cows today might be worth a lot of money, but next year this time, the price might go down, and they could end up upside down if they had bought stock while the price was up. Same for feed, same for crops. One never knew when prices were going to be affected by a drought in Argentina or a virus in Japan.

"But I guess there are some risks worth taking. You weigh the risks, and you decide what you can afford to lose. And then you don't risk any more than that."

"You're saying you did that, and you decided that having a marriage relationship with Deuce wasn't worth losing his friendship over?"

"I don't know. That's what I'm not sure of."

"I guess only you can answer that question."

"That's not very helpful."

"For me, everything that I see in you two says that if you guys decide to take your relationship to the next level, it's going to work. Have you ever kissed him?"

The question seemed to come out of nowhere, and Teagan sat there, her mouth opening and closing.

"Tell you what. I hear Minnie upstairs. She's awake. I'll get her. You go right now, drive over to Deuce's house, and tell him you need to kiss him. After you do that, you come back here and you tell me what you think about taking your relationship to the next level."

"But what if the kiss is awkward? Our friendship will be strained."

"Just tell him you're going to experiment. He'll go along with it. Then if it doesn't work, both of you will brush it under the rug, and you'll pretend it never happened. Plus, he's leaving for two years. It won't be hard to use those two years to forget you ever kissed."

"Do you really think so?"

"It's a risk. Like any risk, there's a lot you can lose, but I think there's a lot more you can gain. I'm pretty sure you'll be happy with the results."

She had always valued Zaylee's opinion. Although, she really didn't have a great track record with men. But still, sometimes a person who made a lot of mistakes had better advice than someone who had never made any.

"You're taking care of Minnie?"

"I am. And while you're at it, you can find out what's going on with her. It seems like we've had her an awful lot lately, and maybe it's time for someone to get involved."

"I hate to have that happen. If someone does, we'll probably end up never seeing her again."

Zaylee nodded, her face reflecting her sadness.

There was always that line. A person wanted to let a parent be a parent and give them a hand, but where was the line? Where did a person need to involve authorities who would take a child and make sure she was cared for properly?

That was one more thing she didn't want to have to think about. That, and whether there would be two cats and a parakeet still in the house when she got back to Sweet Water tonight.

Along with kissing her longtime friend.

It seemed like a good idea, but as she walked out of the house and got in her car, her palms started to sweat and her stomach cramped.

Was this a good idea?

She had decided to do it, so she lifted her chin and pressed down on the accelerator. It seemed like she blinked and she was at Deuce's house, and still she didn't know whether she was making the right decision or not.

Chapter 21

Travis. I need you again.

Travis looked down at his phone at the text from Shanna.

The excitement that he'd always felt when he got a text from her had dimmed in the last few days.

Not that she texted him that much before, but in the last few days, she texted him more than she had since he'd gotten her number last winter at the Christmas dance.

He couldn't believe at the time that she'd given it to him, but now, he almost wished he didn't have it.

He had a feeling he was being used.

She only texted him when she needed to meet the quarterback, Chad, and she wanted him to take her friend away. That's what she needed him for.

But he was in town with his brothers, and she probably knew it.

Despite himself, his fingers responded on their own accord.

The community center?

Yes

Will you be there?

This time there was a pause as he stared at his phone.

Yes.

Alone?

For a bit. If you hurry.

That settled it. He didn't have a five to give to his brothers, to get them to get ice cream, so he told them, "Go to the park. Stay there until I get done with what I need to do. I have enough money in my pocket that we can probably buy a candy bar at the C-Store and share it on the way home."

He had stopped at Sweet Water after he'd dropped his mom off at work in Rockerton. She sometimes allowed him to have the car so he could drive to work at Ford's house, because a coworker would bring her home.

The coworker, a man, would stay overnight at their house, sharing a bedroom with his mom.

Travis didn't like the arrangement, but he did like having a car.

His brothers griped, but they went off in the direction of the park.

As he was hurrying down the street, he saw at the far end of the street a girl struggling with a big hay bale, pulling it off a pickup, and taking it to the back of the house at the end of town.

He recognized the girl. Of course. It was Ellen.

He had known she would be in town and had thought he would help her unload the hay. He'd heard that her uncle asked her to do that while he was showing a horse at the auction barn.

That was a lot of hay for a little girl, and Travis wished he'd have sent his brothers in her direction to help.

Without anything to pay them, they might have griped even more.

For a second, just a second, he considered skipping out on Shanna and helping Ellen.

But there was a small part of him that hoped that this time when Shanna wanted him, she was actually going to do something nice and be there herself.

The memory of the first time he met her, and the kiss that she'd given him, floated up to the top of his mind and pushed the idea of Ellen away.

He headed back between the barbershop and the bakery, walking on the bare ground, fast but not a jog. He had gotten a little bit more reserved since the first time she texted him.

He wasn't sure exactly what she and Chad were doing, but he suspected they weren't conducting business like he originally thought.

Shanna stood where she did before, leaning against the shed with one foot propped against it.

She didn't have her cheerleading uniform on, just short shorts and a halter top. Which was better than the cheerleading uniform. At least in Travis's eyes.

He strode over, noting she was alone.

Maybe his frustration was showing, or maybe he was just being brave, but he didn't hold back the way he might have the first few times she texted him.

He walked straight toward her, slipping an arm around her bare midriff, and pulling her to him, and lowering his head and kissing her the way she had kissed him the first time they met.

She allowed it for several seconds, then she pushed his chest.

"Travis," she said, sounding half annoyed and half amused. "Goodness. What's gotten into you?"

"I think you're using me to watch your friend so you can make out with the football player behind the shed without being interrupted."

"What in the world gave you that idea?" she asked, dismissing him with a glance and letting him know how ridiculous she thought he was.

"Because when you come back to pick up your friend, your lips are all swollen, and he's smirking."

"Really? Are you jealous?" The idea seemed to amuse her, and...something else. Something he wasn't sure about.

"No. I'm just sick of being used."

"I'm not using you. Carrie has the hots for you. I'm doing you a favor. Take advantage of it." She said it like it had been the most obvious thing ever. He hadn't noticed. Carrie hadn't even tried to hold his hand, let alone tried to kiss him the way Shanna had.

Plus, he wasn't interested in Carrie. He was interested in Shanna.

He didn't like the way she could just "give" him to someone else. If he liked her, he wasn't going to share her with all of his friends. No matter how interested they were in her. Did he really have to explain that to her?

Maybe she doesn't like you as much as you think she does. Or want her to.

He didn't like that voice in his head. The one that often told him he was doing something wrong. Something he wanted to do but knew he shouldn't.

He supposed it was his conscience.

"What about you?" he asked, crossing his arms over his chest.

"What about me?" Shanna asked, lowering her eyelids and looking at him underneath her lashes, like she knew exactly what he was saying and liked stringing him along.

"What about you and me?" he clarified, wishing he didn't sound so needy. But Shanna was the one he wanted. Surely once she knew that, she would want him too.

"Oh, my goodness. You're kidding, right?" She looked at him like he was the craziest person she'd ever met.

"What's so wrong about that? You kissed me."

"It meant nothing."

"And just now?"

"Travis, there are classes of people, and some of us are in higher classes than others. You are near the bottom. You and Carrie are perfect for each other. Chad and I, we're in the same class, we know the score, and we can help each other. You remember that, sweetie." She patted his arm. And then, like she hadn't said anything earthshaking to him, she pointed. "Here comes Carrie. Remember what I said. She'll give you whatever you want." She gave him a smile that he really didn't like. "You can thank me later."

With that, she pushed on his elbow, turning him and giving him a little shove in the middle of his back.

He didn't know too much about the ways of women. Other than what his mom did. And he definitely didn't agree with the things that she said sometimes. She had a negative view of life that he thought maybe wasn't accurate.

But maybe it was. Or maybe it was just the way all women were.

Whatever it was, he stopped walking when Carrie stopped in front of him.

"Travis. Do you want to go take a walk down behind the feed store again? Maybe we can find some more tadpoles."

He kinda thought the first time they'd walked there that she wasn't that interested in tadpoles, and knowing what he knew now, he was pretty sure he'd been right. Regardless, he wasn't playing those games anymore. If those were the kind of games women played, he supposed he'd rather just sit out.

"Shanna has been using me to keep you away from her so that she can make out with Chad behind the shed. I'm out."

That was all he said. Maybe Carrie truly did like him. Maybe she wasn't like Shanna after all, but it didn't really matter to him. He was playing in the deep end of the pool, and he was sick of it.

He walked back through the buildings, intent on going back to his brothers, but then he saw Ellen, struggling with another big hay bale.

She was just a tiny little thing, and the bales were definitely too big for her.

When she grew up, she was probably going to be just like Shanna and her friends, and there wasn't too much Travis could do about it.

But he liked Tadgh, and Tadgh loved Ellen. And so far, Ellen had never been anything but kind to him. So, he turned his steps so he was walking toward the pickup, intent on helping Ellen unload.

"I've got these. You go sit down," he said when he got there.

"I appreciate your help. And you can help, but I'll work too," she said, after she blinked at his surprise words.

He didn't argue with her, but grabbed a bale in each hand, and hauled them back, through the front yard and around to the side yard where there was a little lean-to which she had been stacking them beside.

With him helping, it only took ten minutes for them to finish unloading the pickup.

"It was nice of you to help me. Thank you." Ellen spoke without looking at him as she brushed her hands off and then ran them down her shirt and pants, brushing the hayseeds off herself.

"Are you mad at me?" he asked, figuring now was a good time. If she were mad, he shouldn't have helped her to begin with. But he knew he would have anyway.

"No. Why?" she asked, brushing extra hard at her leg, which had no hayseeds on it anymore.

"Because you're not looking at me."

She stopped, straightened, and looked him in the eye. "How about now." She crossed her arms over her chest like she was protecting herself.

"You are. What did I do?"

"Nothing. But I'm pretty sure Shanna is in town. Don't you think you should go help her? Maybe she has some hay bales she's unloading."

His brows furrowed. How did Ellen seem to sense his infatuation with Shanna? Next thing he knew, she was gonna be asking him about Carrie too. "Do you women have some kind of telepathy thing that you use to communicate with each other?"

"No. I saw you."

"Just now?"

"I thought she was in town just now. But no, the other day."

He jerked his head up. Unsure when the other day was but knowing he hadn't been hiding. He hadn't thought he had anything to hide. But now that he knew that Shanna had only been interested in using him, he wished he had been more discreet.

"Well, you've got nothing to worry about. I'll not be seeing her anymore. Not that I was that much to begin with."

"She was using you," Ellen said, sounding wise beyond her twelve years.

Again, he wondered how she knew that. What was it about women and their ability to discern things?

It made him feel stupid. For believing Shanna to begin with.

"Maybe I was using her." He didn't really have anything else to say, so he just said, "Tell your uncle I said hi." He turned around and walked away. Women. They were all the same.

Chapter 22

"That's a good boy. You did a good job," Deuce said as he put the red roan he'd been working with back into the larger corral and walked over to where Jonah and Gideon stood against the fence.

"What did you guys think?" he asked, unsure whether they would be able to tell him anything, since they asked when they stopped in if they could watch and learn.

"I think working with horses takes a lot of patience," Gideon said. "Almost as much as working with a motor, only a motor doesn't move around while I'm trying to work on it."

They laughed together, and Deuce nodded. "That's for sure. Horses do take patience, but they're worth it. It's rewarding."

"I can say the same thing about motors."

"Maybe that's why I like flying. Because it doesn't take a lot of patience. In fact, you have to make a lot of split-second decisions, and you can't wait around." Jonah grinned. "Of course, I appreciate the people who have the patience to work on them so that I can get up in the air without crashing." He slapped Gideon on the back. Then his face sobered. "Maybe that's why my marriage didn't last. I don't have the patience to put up with people when they start doing stupid stuff."

"Include yourself in that."

"I did. I'm probably the one who did the most stupid stuff in my marriage. And a lot of the time, I took my irritation and lack of patience out on her."

Deuce wasn't sure what to say. He'd never been in that position, but he did know that when he started to get short tempered, it was usually his own fault. Teagan didn't let him get away with it though. She called him out on it, and normally she had them both laughing by the time they were done talking.

He missed her today. She was usually hanging on the rail while he worked with the horses, if she could get the time off. But she was watching Minnie for him today instead.

"You guys didn't have to come the whole way over here. When I texted you and said I needed to talk to you guys, I thought I could just do it over the phone."

"We wanted to see you work anyway. If we're going to be working with horses and using them on the farm, we ought to get used to being around them."

"It doesn't hurt to watch the master," Gideon added.

"I don't know that I'm a master, but I have successfully trained a lot of horses. Not thousands. But hundreds maybe."

Now that he was older, he wished he'd kept track. But it never seemed important. He didn't even have records, other than what he had to keep for tax purposes.

"But, speaking of, what was it you needed to say?"

"I told you guys that I'd be working on horses for you, and I gave you a timeframe. But something came up with my parents' business, and it might take me a little longer than what I thought. I'll have a few weeks before I have to go, but I'll need to live in Fargo, and I'll only be able to come home and work with horses on Saturdays and Sundays. So, I think I told you eight weeks, but it's probably going to be more like four months."

The men nodded and looked at each other before Jonah looked back and shrugged. "We heard you were the best. If it takes a little longer than what you thought it was going to, we're still with you, unless you want us to go somewhere else?"

"No. I just didn't want to give you a promise and then not be able to keep it. I wanted to let you know as soon as I knew that things weren't going to work out the way I thought."

"Life seldom does. Appreciate the heads-up. But we're not really in a rush."

"I've been wondering what you guys are doing over there," Deuce said, not wanting to come right out and ask but thinking that they could tell him whatever they felt like it was okay for him to know.

Gideon grinned. "We're not growing marijuana if that's what you're asking."

Deuce lifted both hands. "I wasn't asking, because I hadn't even thought about it. But thanks for letting me know. That's a relief."

They all laughed together, with Gideon saying, "But I've heard it's a good cash crop."

"Does it grow in North Dakota?" Deuce asked, more to make conversation than because he really cared. He certainly wasn't planning on growing any.

"I don't know. That's not something we would ever look into growing anyway. We're just a bunch of Air Force dudes, and we decided to buy a ranch together. Ground is a lot cheaper up here in North Dakota, although we understand it's a lot harder to make a living up here as well. That's why we all went in together on this ranch. And that's why we chose Sweet Water. There's the Olympic training center that's going up, so there'll be people around, for businesses, and there's also going to be land available with people coming in and heading out when they can't make it."

Jonah looked serious. "Not that we're banking on people going bankrupt, but it's just a fact up here. We did our research."

Deuce nodded. He knew plenty of people who came in with big hopes and dreams, liking the cheap land but not banking on the brutal winters and the short summers. "You have to be pretty hardy to be able to make it up here."

"Well, we got the hardiness thing down. And we're not afraid to work either. And we figure with all of us throwing in and with us all having jobs off the ranch, we think we can make it. At least, we'll make the payments."

"And some of us are trading our airplanes in for horses." Gideon smirked.

"Speak for yourself. I'm keeping a firm hold on my wings."

"If you want to work on the ranch, you're going to need something a little different than a plane," Deuce quipped. The men laughed again.

The more he talked to these guys, the more he liked them. And the more he appreciated the fact that he was going to have great neighbors.

"I agree with you, and I think you're smart to have a job off the farm. At least at first. Pretty much everyone I know ranches and does something else on the side. Whether it's going to farmers markets or training horses." He nodded at the paddock where his horses milled around. "Or my parents have a wholesale construction business, which is what I'm going to be doing in Fargo. Their warehouse there isn't doing very well, and they want me to take it over and see if I can't turn things around."

"That's pretty impressive, you train horses, and you're going to do the warehousing on the side?"

"That's just it, the horses are going to be on the side, and I also do the IT work too." He didn't mean to brag, but he figured he'd throw that out there, just so the guys knew. Sometimes people needed help with their computers, and he wouldn't be against trading vehicle maintenance for computer maintenance, if they needed it.

The guys didn't say anything, but he figured they were probably tucking that information away the same as he was.

From what he'd heard in town, none of the guys were married, so he didn't ask about that. Not like he normally would have anyway. It wasn't something that typically came up in a man's conversation.

But he knew if Teagan were to find out he'd had a talk with the men, she'd want to know.

They left a few minutes later, and Deuce had gotten another horse out of the bigger paddock and led it into the arena where he planned to do some groundwork with it when a pickup came rumbling up.

It wasn't one that he recognized right off, although it looked familiar, and he figured it was someone from Sweet Water.

When it stopped and Mr. Marshall got out, he realized why it was familiar.

Mr. Blaze and Mr. Junior got out on the other side, and all three men walked over to the arena gate, where they stopped, propping their feet on one rail, their hands hanging over the top board, their canes dangling loosely.

Deuce had been working on ground tying that particular horse, so he let the reins drop and walked over.

"Nice day for a drive," he said to the men standing there.

"It sure is," Mr. Marshall said, looking up at the sky like he hadn't realized it until Deuce had said something.

That was odd in itself, because pretty much everyone in town knew exactly what the weather was doing on any given day. That was the main topic of conversation after the price of corn and wheat and beef.

"Is there something I can help you with?" he asked, when all the men just kind of stood there looking at him.

"We're looking for a man." Mr. Junior finally spoke up from the end.

Deuce tilted his head, scrunched his brows up, and said, "Somebody rob the C-Store?" Why would they be looking for a man? Would they have some kind of description?

He was about to ask when Blaze held up his hand. "No, no, no. You misunderstand. We've got a lady who needs a husband, and we're looking for a man for her."

Deuce stood there, his mouth open. He managed to shut it, but it fell right back open again.

"You want a husband for a woman?" he said the words slowly, choosing them carefully, but his question still didn't actually ask what he wanted to ask. But he didn't know how to phrase what he wanted to say. He supposed he should ask if the men were feeling okay. Or if the heat had made one of them feel a little wobbly, and maybe they should sit down in the shade for a bit.

"Yeah. That's what we need. We got a single woman in town, and we made a deal with her daughter that we'd find her a husband. And you're at the top of our list."

"Me?" he asked, incredulous. Maybe he should be a little bit pleased that he was at the top of anyone's list to be a husband, but... "I'm not really looking for a husband job. But if you have a horse you want trained—"

The men shook their heads sadly. "No. We don't need a horse trainer. We need a husband."

"Well, I'm sorry. But..." He didn't know what to say. So finally he just said the words that seemed to want to tumble out of his mouth anyway. "Actually I'm thinking about seeing if Teagan wants me to apply for the job with her. She isn't the woman you're looking for a husband for, is she?"

He thought they had said something about doing it for a woman's daughter, so it probably wasn't Teagan, but he could hope. If the men were trying to match him up with someone, and they accidentally matched him up with Teagan, it would take a lot of the responsibility off his shoulders.

Not that he was necessarily looking to get out of it, he just...didn't know how to handle her. Well, he knew how to handle her as a friend, but he wasn't sure how to take what felt like a huge, giant step into the unknown romantic kind of relationship.

He enjoyed holding her hand, hugging her, but anything more seemed a lot more risky, and neither one of them had said anything about it today.

Maybe she decided that she didn't want to. And he would have to respect that, but he hated to ask, because then his hopes would be dashed.

"I don't suppose you know anyone who is looking for that type of position?" Junior said, fingering his white beard thoughtfully.

"Nope." Then Deuce stopped short. "Well, maybe I do." He thought about the men who had just been there. There wasn't any woman out there, and they were all living there by themselves. Maybe one of them would want to get married. Or at the very least, maybe one of them would want to hire someone to cook for them.

"You know the Sweet Briar Ranch?" He looked at the men, who all nodded. Everyone knew the Sweet Briar Ranch. No one had lived on it for a while, and the whole town had been abuzz when the men had bought it.

"Well, there's a whole bunch of men out there. I think one of those men might possibly be looking for a husband job."

"I don't suppose you know any of them?" Junior said. "I mean, I've seen them around town, know their names, but I haven't been able to get much background information out of them."

"Hate to match anyone up when I don't know the person that I'm matching her with. And we got a nice girl. We need to find her a husband who works for her."

Deuce didn't usually do this, but he lowered his voice, after looking around. "You might want to talk to Miss Charlene in town. She had been doing a lot of matchmaking the last couple years."

"Yeah. We've already thought of that. But rumor has it around town that she quit."

"She might have passed the baton to someone else." Deuce didn't know what else to say. He certainly wasn't going to take over any matchmaking duties. He couldn't even get his own self matched. He certainly didn't have any idea of how to match anyone else.

"I suppose you might be right. I wonder where I could find that out?" Junior said thoughtfully.

"Ask Miss Charlene."

"As I understand it, she never did come right out and admit that she was matchmaking. Although, I did hear some rumors about last Christmas."

Deuce had heard the same rumors, whether or not they were true, and whether or not it was an accident that Miss Charlene and Mr. Charlie had gotten locked in the Sunday school room, he wasn't sure. He did know that they had a pretty fast wedding.

Still, all of his speculation would just be gossip, so he let that comment go.

"If you don't ask her, you won't know. Otherwise, I'll keep an eye out, but I really can't help you out."

"You're sure you're not up for it?"

"No. I think I might say something to Teagan the next time I see her."

"You guys are probably made for each other anyway. All I ever see you doing is laughing and having fun together. Of course, you get married and all that goes down the drain, and you end up snapping and sniffing and fighting with each other the same way every other married couple ever does." Marshall shook his head, like the idea of people being happily married was a myth.

"I think I'm gonna turn that myth on its head. And you'll see, Teagan and I are going to keep laughing from now through the next fifty years. You mark my words."

Deuce knew his words were rather brave, considering he hadn't even talked the girl into doing what he wanted, but he knew for a fact that if he and Teagan got married, they would be happy together. He would make sure of it.

Of course, their earlier conversation came back to him, where a person couldn't determine what anyone else did. They could only determine what they themselves did.

Still, he was as confident as he could be with Teagan. They'd been friends for almost twenty years, and both of them had always thought about the other person first. Even when they were younger. He had no reason to think that it was going to change now. Still, he appreciated the wisdom of the older men.

"Sometimes you young whippersnappers have a lot to learn," Marshall said, shaking his head at what he probably supposed to be his youthful naiveté.

"If you don't believe in relationships lasting, why are you trying to find a man for your single woman?" Deuce asked with a grin. The men weren't making sense.

"We made a deal," Blaze began.

"Shh!" Junior said immediately, shutting him down. He laughed a little, uncomfortably, as he looked back at Deuce. "It's not really something we can talk about."

Deuce shrugged. "That's fine. Not a big deal. I'll keep an eye out, and I guess I'll let you know if I see any guys that suit your preferences."

The men nodded, made a few comments about the weather, and then turned to go.

Deuce watched them thoughtfully. Normally he would turn back to his work without a second glance. But he wondered again at what they had said and how it jibed with his conversation with Teagan.

Then, something he hadn't thought about before, but something that he knew instinctively, hit his mind.

He didn't know what would happen tomorrow, but he had a God who did. He could take a step forward, in faith, as long as he was sure that God was guiding his path. If he was doing what the Lord wanted, it didn't matter whether his wife stayed with him or didn't. Whether she kept her word or whether she didn't. God knew. And

God would take care of him, allowing him to go through whatever trials God felt he needed to in order to become a better man.

He knew that, just as well as he knew that it was up to him to try to do right. And he couldn't make anyone else, not his parents, not his sisters, not even Teagan, and certainly if they had children, he couldn't make his kids do right either. All he could do was the best that he could do at doing what God wanted him to do, and trust that God would take care of him, even if God allowed him to go through fiery trials.

He thought of a verse from a great hymn and hummed a few bars. *When through fiery trials thy pathways shall lie, My grace all sufficient shall be thy supply.*

He almost turned back around to walk to the horse, when a car came around the bend and passed the pickup that was just leaving.

He didn't have any trouble recognizing that car. It was Teagan's.

Chapter 23

Teagan's hands gripped the steering wheel so hard her knuckles were white. Sweat made them slippery, but she held tight as her car pulled to a stop by the corral where Deuce stood, hands in his pockets, waiting.

Could she really go through with this?

Dread balled in her stomach, but coupled with that was an excitement that she couldn't deny. If she did this, it would be the single most crazy thing she'd ever done in her life before, but it could also be the absolute very best.

The idea of kissing Deuce, of being more with him, of having him beside her for the rest of her life, of being his wife, of having children and a home together filled her with so much joy and longing, she almost could forget that he might not want any of it.

He might be content with their friendship and feel the idea of kissing her was...repulsive.

She swallowed.

"Hey," Deuce said, his head in her open window. "Are you okay?"

Drat. She had wanted to be out of the car. It was going to be awkward to step out with him right there and try to kiss him immediately.

"Teagan? What happened?" he said, his voice holding threads of panic. He knew her so well. He could tell that she was contemplating a life-changing decision, or knew something was up. "How can I help?"

He bent down, his head in beside her, his eyes holding worry, his brows creased. His hand landed on her shoulder, warm and firm and comforting.

Her heart twisted, a little painful, but mostly good and warm.

His face was so close she could see his stubble clearly, feel his breath on her cheek. She could lean forward and touch her lips to the side of his face, touch his skin.

Her hand came up without her meaning for it to and she stroked the side of his face.

"Please tell me," he whispered.

She took a breath.

"I can't stand to see you like this. Tell me." His words held pleading and pain. Even though he didn't know what was causing her distress, he hurt with her. She loved that.

Maybe it was the idea that he would share her pain, would help her however he could, would be in her corner without even knowing what they were fighting; he would fight with her.

Or maybe it was her faith in what they could have overcoming her fear in stepping out.

Or maybe it was just time.

"I love you." Her words were soft, breathy.

That wasn't the way she wanted to say it.

"I love you." That was a little better, stronger.

"I love you, Deuce." She forced herself to look into his eyes, to let him see the truth in hers, to make herself vulnerable, to risk everything, because what she wanted and could have with this man was worth giving herself for.

"You know I love you too, Teagan," Deuce said, his brows still down, his face still showing concern and confusion.

He didn't understand what she was saying, what she wanted.

The kiss. She needed to kiss him. That would make him understand.

"Deuce, I..." She slid her hand around his neck. His eyes darkened, but when she tugged he didn't move.

"Teagan?"

Maybe she could try again with words, show him with her tone of voice. "Deuce, I love you."

She didn't have any other words, couldn't get her brain to come up with anything that made sense, couldn't string the words together.

Her hand ran over his cheek. The touch of a lover, not a friend. Could he tell?

His eyes flickered.

"I love you. Love your humor and your smile. The crazy way you compliment me. Your patience with your horses and your loyalty to your family. I love that you'll go anywhere with me, do anything, and have fun and laugh. Whether we're hunting for a cat or going through an old house. I love that you'll protect me. That you'll leave whatever you're doing to come be with me so the neighbor won't bother me. You'll stand with me, stay with me, cook with me and hang out, content to just be with me."

"You'll do all that for me."

"Because I love you."

"And I love you. We've already said that."

"Deuce, my hands are trembling and I'm scared to death, but I want to kiss you. I thought I'd just try it and see, but my stomach is in knots and my heart is pounding in my chest and I can hardly breathe. I don't want to try it, I want to do it, because kissing you is all I can think of. I want-"

Her voice cut off in a short gasp as his mouth came down on hers.

He finally understood what she was saying, what she wanted, and from the tightening of his hand, moving around her shoulders and pulling her closer, careful at first, then the more firm and deliberate moving of his mouth on hers, she knew he got her, and, better yet, wanted the same thing, if his low groan and the tilting of his head to fit their mouths more closely together was any indication.

Her eyes closed and her hands pulled him closer and her entire body felt hot and cold and soft and frozen and shifting and solid.

He pulled back and she clung, not wanting to end the kiss, not wanting to let him go. "Teagan? I've wanted this for so long."

She couldn't help it. That made her lips quirk up. "Why was I the one who finally said something?"

"I guess you're braver than I am." His breath fanned across her face and his hand gently pushed her hair back, his fingers lingering in it like he loved the way she felt and didn't want to pull his hand away.

"Maybe I'm just better at taking risks?"

"Probably. Or maybe I didn't want to kiss you and only get to do it once."

"Oh?"

"Because you'd tell me that you didn't like me like that."

"You were afraid of that, too?"

"So afraid. I decided I'd rather not lose you and never have everything I wanted."

"And I decided the opposite."

They laughed a little, then he sobered. "I'm glad you made that decision." He paused. "Are you sure?"

"I'm sure."

"Where do we go from here?" he asked, his face bending closer, like he wanted to kiss her again, but knew they needed to talk.

"I guess we are going to Fargo?" she asked, breathless. "And, not to change the subject, but I didn't know kissing my best friend would make it so hard to breathe."

"I'm glad you're having trouble with that, too." He smiled a little, touching the side of her mouth with his lips. "So, you're going to Fargo with me?"

"Yes. If you want me to."

"I do. I want you to go...as my wife."

She blinked, pulling back. "Wife?"

"Is that too much of a stretch?" He looked into her eyes, then held her gaze as his lips touched the corner of her mouth again. "You don't think I go around kissing women like this without having serious intentions?"

"I think the kissing was my idea."

"It was. But I can get onboard with your ideas, especially good ones like this, pretty fast when I need to."

She laughed, kissing him back, getting a little distracted when he turned his head and their lips met and tangled.

"So, you're onboard and you proposed already?"

"I have less than a month. I want you with me." He slid his thumb over her cheek and kissed her nose, then moved to the side of her jaw. "You've had a couple of decades to get to know me. Think you can put up with me as your husband? Or do you need some time to think about it?"

"If you can put up with me, I can put up with you. Although I think I'm getting the better end of the bargain."

"We can argue about that if you want, because I disagree."

She smiled. "I think I might look forward to our arguments from now on. I can think of some satisfying ways to end them. Ways that involve kissing."

They grinned, new and exciting knowledge in their eyes as they shared a sweet look. Her toes tingled.

"I think we could get married today if you want."

"I want. Maybe we should make sure we have two cats and a parakeet before we head in to the courthouse and get ourselves a license?"

That sounded so final. So...soon. She swallowed. This was Deuce. They did everything together, including getting married. How fun to embark on that new adventure with her best friend.

Before she could say anything, he said, "Maybe you want more time?"

"I want to be married. Now that we made that decision, that's what I want." The words were true.

"But?"

Ha. She should have known he'd know there was something else.

"Can we wait until tomorrow? Let this settle a bit first?"

"Practice kissing?"

"Yeah. Practice kissing. Practice being...more than friends?"

"I'm in."

"And I'm in with checking on the cats. And the bird. And anything else you want to check on."

"I just want to be with you. The idea of leaving and not seeing you every day was killing me." He put his forehead on hers. "I'm so glad you came over and did this today."

"It took you a little bit to catch on."

"You took me by surprise." He grinned. "But I'm all caught up and ready to move ahead. I do, by the way, think this is the best idea you've ever had."

"Kissing you? I agree."

"Marrying me."

"That was your idea. And I think that was the best one you've ever had."

"You would know. You've been with me through all my ideas, good and bad."

"And I'll be here for all of the rest of them, for the rest of our lives."

"I'll feel better about that when I have a ring on your finger." He froze. "I need a ring!"

"Maybe that's what we can do after we find our animals. Get rings."

"You are just full of good ideas today." They grinned at each other. "I think more kissing might be another good idea."

"I agree."

And it was a long time before they found any cats.

Chapter 24

Deuce sat on Miss April's porch swing, gently swaying, holding Teagan's hand in his, playing with the ring he'd put on her finger less than two weeks ago.

The move from best friends to more had been almost seamless. His worries about ruining their friendship seemed almost silly now.

"What time did you say Miss April was supposed to get here?" he asked, not impatient. He didn't mind doing anything as long as Teagan was with him.

"She said Edgar and she should be arriving anytime." Teagan's quiet voice held contentment.

They hadn't been able to go anywhere for a honeymoon while she'd been responsible for watching Miss April's animals, but tomorrow they planned to head to Montana and spend a few days at a secluded cabin in the mountains. Deuce had to admit he was looking forward to spending even more time with his wife.

They were quiet for a bit. The occasional shout of kids playing reached them, as well as the hum of a car and the creaking of the springs holding the swing. Someone was grilling and the scent drifted down, making his stomach rumble.

"Want to find something to eat?" Teagan asked.

"I think that's Miss April, right now," Deuce said, as a car pulled to a stop in front of the house.

"Perfect timing. We'll be eating in just a few minutes."

"She's always hungry."

"I am not!" she exclaimed, then added. "Just most of the time."

"Ha. I knew you'd eventually admit it."

"Admit what?"

"That you eat more than I do."

"I do not."

"You do."

"Do not."

"Sounds like nothing has changed around here." Miss April interrupted them. Deuce had been so focused on Teagan, he'd totally forgotten about her.

They stood up from the swing.

"Oh. A few things have changed," Teagan said with a smile and a wink at him.

He grinned back, holding his hand out to Mr. Edgar. "Welcome back."

"Good to be home," Edgar said, hefting a suitcase up the stairs with him.

"How did you make out with?" Miss April asked, looking between the two of them.

"Your cats are fine."

"My cats?" Miss April said with a confused look before her eyes widened and she said, "Oh. Yes. My cats. They're good?"

"Yep." Teagan hurried over to the door, but Deuce beat her and opened it for her. She gave him a grin as she waited for Miss April to go in first. Teagan followed her in.

Elizabeth meowed and rubbed against Teagan's leg.

"Oh, Cordelia!" Miss April said, bending down and seeming to remember she loved her cat as she patted the top of its head.

"Oh, no!" Teagan said, dismayed. Deuce went over and put his arm around her. "I've been calling them by the wrong names all this time. I could have sworn you said that was Elizabeth."

Miss April blinked like she wasn't sure if she had said that or not. Then she straightened. "It's okay. We all get confused sometimes. Elizabeth is the one that is shy and doesn't come right away."

"But I thought..." Teagan started.

"Actually, once they got used to us, both of them were fine," Deuce said, squeezing Teagan's shoulder and drawing her closer to him. He didn't think he'd ever get tired of holding her.

"Of course. That's what they always do," Miss April said. "Now." The insecurity left her eyes and they got a shrewd look as she glanced between Deuce and Teagan. "Looks like you two might be..."

"Married?" Deuce supplied for her. "Yep. Can't believe you didn't hear that from someone before you arrived home."

"Married? You're kidding! This went better than I expected! I had no idea you two would work so quickly, but that was my plan all along –" She seemed to realize what she was saying and stopped abruptly.

"Your plan all along?" Teagan asked slowly. Not offended, just confused.

Deuce felt the exact same way.

Miss April hesitated. Then she looked between the two of them. "You're really married?"

"Yes?" Deuce answered, unsure what was up, but as long as Teagan was okay, he was too.

"Then I guess I can tell you..." She sighed. "The cats aren't mine. I borrowed them from Miss June. And the parakeet is Miss Helen's."

"What?" Teagan exclaimed.

Deuce had to admit he couldn't understand it, either.

"I wanted to give you two an excuse to be together, so I had to borrow cats for you to pet sit for me. Also, Edger and I didn't go any farther than his Aunt Bertha's cabin outside of Rockerton. It was all I could do to get that man to leave Sweet Water." Miss April harrumphed. "The internet in that old place is terrible, but the TV worked, so he was happy."

Deuce laughed.

Teagan said, "But why?"

"I paid Gerald to come over and act all stalkerish so you'd feel uncomfortable and I figured that would get Deuce here."

"Gerald...was acting?" Teagan asked in amazement. Then she shook her head. "He was pretty good. Very menacing and more than a little scary."

"But he didn't hurt you." Miss April's tone was confident.

"No. Of course not. But...you're right. I felt much better when Deuce was here."

Deuce smiled at that, his heart warming. He loved that his presence had made her feel safe. Of course, Miss April had manipulated them, but he could hardly be upset about that. There was no way he'd be upset with anything that helped Teagan and he get to where they were – happily married. *Very* happily married.

He smiled at the thought and wondered how much longer they'd need to stand around and talk. He wouldn't mind getting his wife home and being alone with her for a while.

If Teagan was upset about what Miss April was done, she didn't look like it. He highly doubted it since she would think the same way he did – that it got them together, so it was a good thing.

They chatted for a bit more, but Teagan seemed as eager as he was to leave, so, when Edgar went out for their second suitcase, they followed him out and bade them farewell.

They were in Deuce's pickup before Teagan spoke. "Can you believe she wanted us to be together so much she borrowed cats and faked an anniversary trip?"

"They didn't really fake the trip. They just didn't go where they said they were going."

"Same thing." Teagan shook her head.

He didn't want to argue with that.

"Whatever she did. I appreciate it. It brought you to your senses."

"Me? What about you?"

"I was just waiting for that to finally happen."

She gave him a side glance. "Like you knew all along?"

"That we were meant to be together?" He was going to give her a flippant answer, but he stopped. He had a great rapport with Teagan, but she loved the pretty words, too. He had been trying to do a better job of giving them to her. "You probably knew before I did. I just knew I didn't want to do anything without you. I'm not sure why I would think kissing would be the exception to that, but thankfully, you are braver than me." He paused. "Although, I think I'm addicted now."

"Addicted?"

"To kissing you."

She tilted her head. "I think I like that." Her look became thoughtful. "You know, the summer festival isn't far away. I wonder if Cormac and Brooklyn might find out the same thing?"

"That they're addicted to kissing you? I hope not," Deuce teased and was rewarded with a laugh from his wife.

"No, goofball. That they enjoy kissing each other. I mean, after all, aren't you the one who said that if they'd just act like they liked each other, the town would stop pushing them together? It worked for us."

"You could be right." Deuce didn't really care about Cormac and Brooklyn, although he did feel like everyone in the world should have someone who loved them and had their back like Teagan loved him and had his. "I love you," he said.

Her eyes widened in surprise.

"That was a subject change."

"I just wanted you to know in case you'd forgotten since I said it last."

"Keep reminding me." She smiled. "Also, I love you, too." Her look was soft, but then she added, "And I kissed you first!"

He almost said he would kiss her last, but he didn't want to think about the end. They were at the beginning and he just wanted to enjoy every second he could with her. Someday they'd be old together, but that was a long way away. In the meantime, he just wanted to savor a life lived with his best friend.

And kissing. He also wanted kissing.

Enjoy this preview of *Just a Cowboy's Enemy*, just for you!

Just a Cowboy's Enemy

Chapter 1

"I would prefer not to be in the kissing booth."

Brooklyn Lepley knew her words were not nearly strong enough. She should have said firmly, *I will not do the kissing booth.*

But it was always so hard to look into Miss Charlene's eyes and turn her down for anything. Mostly because she knew Miss Charlene would do anything for Brooklyn. And had.

When their oldest sister Cheyenne had been dying of cancer, the ladies of the town had rallied around their family, cooking meals, taking turns helping out at the house, cleaning, driving, getting the kids off to school, helping with homework, even making sure the ranch kept running.

They had fundraisers multiple times over the years to help with hospital bills and co-pays and expenses.

Brooklyn looked down at the floor.

Cheyenne hadn't made it, but part of Cheyenne's legacy was how it had taught Brooklyn that being a part of a community was not something that a person took for granted.

Part of not taking that for granted was pulling her weight, whatever she needed to.

Even if it meant being in the kissing booth for the annual Sweet Water Summer Festival.

Except, she just couldn't do it.

Miss Charlene sighed but didn't look like she was judging her or even upset. She simply looked at Miss April sadly, and said, "The kissing booth is usually our biggest moneymaker, but it's the one thing I always have trouble getting people to do. I guess... I guess we just won't have it this year."

Her eyes seemed to slide to Brooklyn's, and if it were anyone other than Miss Charlene, Brooklyn would have said that there was some kind of calculating thought in her gaze, but it just couldn't be.

Miss April said, "That's too bad. And we were going to send the proceeds of the kissing booth to the Fargo Children's Cancer Memorial Hospital." Miss Charlene and Miss April sadly shook their heads. Brooklyn might have been imagining it, but she almost thought that Miss Helen and Miss June each wiped a tear from the corner of their eye.

She almost crossed her arms over her chest and accused the ladies of laying it on really thick, because they were making her feel guilty.

They didn't have to say Cheyenne's name in order to make Brooklyn feel like she owed the town a lot more than two hours in the kissing booth. The problem was, she knew, without a shadow of a doubt, who she would be in the kissing booth with.

Cormac.

There was no way she was going to be in the kissing booth with Cormac. She refused.

Miss April lifted her head, and either she had something stuck in her eye, or they were watering.

Brooklyn tried to tell herself they weren't watering.

"If you change your mind, go ahead and let us know. But otherwise, we just won't be able to do it this year."

Brooklyn tried to steel her heart. She wasn't going to be persuaded into spending two hours with Cormac just because the ladies made her feel guilty and also because of Cheyenne's memory shimmering in the back of her head, seeming to tell her that life was not about making herself happy or about being selfish.

"All right, I'll do it." She closed her eyes, the words coming out quickly before she changed her mind. Or before she walked out.

If the ladies were anyone else, they might have said something along the lines, "No. You said you weren't, and we know you don't want to, so don't worry about it."

But that's not what the ladies did.

Miss Charlene clapped her hands, and Miss April said immediately, "Thank you very much. We'll put your name down. I know there's going to be a big crowd this year, and this will be huge."

Yeah. People always came if they knew that Brooklyn and Cormac were going to be together.

They both had been assigned to the kissing booth three years ago, but Cormac had mysteriously developed double pneumonia right in the middle of summer. Funny, because she had seen him the week before the festival and the week after, and he looked healthy as a horse both times.

She could only surmise that the reason he hadn't gone to the summer festival, and had backed out of the kissing booth, was because he didn't want to be with her.

Well, the feeling was mutual. Plus, she was the one with all the grievances.

"We don't want to keep you. You go ahead and do what you were planning on doing. Delivering groceries or something, right?" Miss Charlene said, almost as though she knew Brooklyn was on the verge of changing her mind and telling them she wouldn't do it and wanted to show her out the door before she could.

That was probably a good strategy. As long as it had taken Brooklyn to actually get here with the intention of telling them she couldn't, she'd never make it back in before the festival started.

And unlike some people, once she said she would do something, she would do it, unless there was a very good reason why she wouldn't.

She wouldn't make up some ridiculous explanation like double pneumonia.

"Yeah. I was delivering groceries to Mrs. Reinhart."

Maybe her voice sounded a little fatalistic. Like she knew her goose was cooked and there was nothing she could do about it.

After all, the shimmering picture of Cheyenne in the back of her head wouldn't allow her to open her mouth and tell these ladies that she wasn't going to do the most profitable thing at the summer festival, wasn't going to allow them to make money to send to the Fargo Children's Cancer Memorial Hospital, wasn't going to pay back the town for everything they had done for them over the years.

Of course she was going to do it.

Even if she had to hold her nose the entire time.

As well she might, since she didn't know how else she was going to get through two hours in the kissing booth with Cormac Henderson.

She waved at the ladies as she walked out the door, still a little upset that they manipulated her into doing what they wanted her to do, but knowing she would never hold a grudge.

She was well aware that the ladies had a reputation for matchmaking, but Miss Charlene had seemed to retire after her marriage to Charlie, and while the Piece Makers still met in the basement of the church, it wasn't the same.

Things changed, people moved on, and that was life.

Miss April, along with Miss Helen and Miss June, met at the community center to do crafts, and rumor had it, they talked about how to have good marriages and be good wives.

Miss Charlene dropped in once in a while to add her wisdom to the discussion.

They were no longer matchmaking.

She almost laughed at that idea. Because if they were, they were totally wasting their time on her and Cormac. There was no future in matchmaking for anyone who thought that was a good match.

It was a beautiful day out, and she decided she wasn't going to drive her car down the street to Mrs. Reinhart's house but simply grab the groceries out of the back and walk them down.

As she rooted around in the trunk, she realized she had underestimated the number of groceries she had bought.

There were ten bags, which she could easily hold in each hand, but there was also a box of tissues and a large twelve-roll package of paper towels.

With five bags in each hand, a box in one, and the paper towels in the other, she would look ridiculous as she walked down the street, but she'd already decided she wasn't driving, so she hefted the things up, balancing the paper towels with the side of her head and the box of tissues with her chin.

She nodded at her sister Teagan and her new husband, Deuce, whom she passed as they walked into the diner. They commented on what a beautiful morning it was, and she concurred.

"Do you need help with those?" Teagan asked as Deuce held the door open for her.

"No. I'm exercising." She grinned, to make her statement a fun one rather than looking like she was struggling. It really was good exercise, although she hadn't deliberately set out for that reason.

Still, she loved the challenge, and she definitely was going to make it. The bags were heavy but not unbearable, and it would feel good to get everything there in one load. Challenging herself to do something a little bit hard.

Maybe she'd missed the fact that one of the bags had a hole in them, or maybe the weight from the cans of diced tomatoes was too much for the plastic, but she had barely taken another fifty steps toward Mrs. Reinhart's house when one of the bags broke, the cans spilling out and rolling down the sidewalk.

She'd been pretty confident not two minutes before, now she was kicking herself.

Using her feet, she tried to stop all the cans from rolling toward the road, since she could hear a truck rumbling down Main Street behind her.

It wouldn't be coming fast, nothing went fast through Sweet Water, but she didn't want to lose any of her cans, if she could help it.

Allowing the box of tissues and the paper towels to drop to the ground, she let go of the bags in one hand and ran after one can that must have hit a hill or slope in the sidewalk since it was going faster than all the other ones and was on a diagonal to drop off the edge of the sidewalk and onto the road.

Thankfully, the truck passed before the can dropped.

Maybe her concentration was a little bit off, or maybe she wasn't as coordinated as she used to be, but as she got close to the can, with her fingers just a few inches from it, she ended up kicking it with her foot, so it sailed off in an arc and landed in the middle of the street.

By that time, she was going too fast to stop, and she ran out after it.

Foolishly, it turned out, since the Highlander cow that had been running loose in Sweet Water since last winter was apparently following the truck.

Maybe the truck was hauling feed or something. She wasn't sure why the cow would be chasing it, but she hadn't heard its hooves pounding on the pavement until it was too late.

Well, not quite too late, since strong arms wrapped around her and lifted her off her feet, swinging her to the left.

Just in time, since the Highlander's fur brushed her arm as it went past.

She wasn't quite sure how the horns missed them, but they did.

Maybe it was a tension relief, but she laughed a little as her feet settled back on the sidewalk and she turned, a smile on her face and words of appreciation on her lips for whoever had been more aware of her surroundings than she was and had rescued her from being run over by a cow.

That would be something she would never live down in a small town. She would always be known as that girl who had gotten run over by a cow and ended up in the hospital for three days with broken ribs and lacerations from the encounter.

The joke about saving her reputation died on her lips as she saw just who had rescued her.

Cormac Henderson.

Pick up your copy of *Just a Cowboy's Enemy* by Jessie Gussman today!

A Gift from Jessie

View this code through your smart phone camera to be taken to a page where you can download a FREE ebook when you sign up to get updates from Jessie Gussman! Find out why people say, "Jessie's is the only newsletter I open and read" and "You make my day brighter. Love, love, love reading your newsletters. I don't know where you find time to write books. You are so busy living life. A true blessing." and "I know from now on that I can't be drinking my morning coffee while reading your newsletter – I laughed so hard I sprayed it out all over the table!"

Printed in Great Britain
by Amazon